ENJOY !

Rolicking City Police

Blue Deceit

Lou Morissette

iUniverse, Inc.
New York   Bloomington

Rolicking City Police
Blue Deceit

iUniverse books may be ordered through booksellers or by contacting:

iUniverse
1663 Liberty Drive
Bloomington, IN 47403
www.iuniverse.com
1-800-Authors (1-800-288-4677)

ISBN: 978-1-4502-2401-7 (pbk)
ISBN: 978-1-4502-2402-4 (cloth)
ISBN: 978-1-4502-2403-1 (ebk)

Printed in the United States of America

iUniverse rev. date: 5/11/2010

Please check out rolickingcitypolice.com! I'd also appreciate it, if you could pass on your thoughts: rolickingcitypolice@gmail.com

This story is written for police officers everywhere that continue to do the right thing at the ongoing expense of their personal lives.
To my wife Marie and daughter Claire, you are my daily inspiration!
(Claire, you can't read this book until you are 14!)
To Mom, who was never without a novel in hand—I know you're reading!

Most Importantly:
Half of the royalties from book sales will be donated to "A Port in the Storm" Winnipeg, Manitoba, Canada which is a not for profit agency. "A Port in the Storm" provides family accommodation and support for rural Manitoba residents undergoing medical treatment in Winnipeg. Your support through the purchase of this book is greatly appreciated. It only has to matter once, that you cared so much.

http://aportinthestorm.ca/
A Port in the Storm
161 Rue Grandin
Winnipeg, Manitoba
R2H 0A8

Your generosity is greatly appreciated!

Preface

Now that we have gotten the dreaded "Disclaimer" out of the way, there may very well be some hybrid characters in the book that could "appear" real. These characters appear so realistic that you may convince yourself that you are them! Don't fall into this trap. Over the course of my 26 years with the RCMP and working with outside agencies, you meet every permutation of law enforcement officer known to mankind. There will always be, to their credit, a Kate and Earl out there in some form or another. These types of police officers are, more aptly, defined as hard working and relentless in their pursuit of bad guys. Like all solid people, they have character flaws which only tend to better highlight their intrinsic "good."

This book was written with the average cop in mind. Senior police managers all too often forget the plight of the working cop. Sometimes you can get lucky and the strength of parody shines through. The RCP Department could be anywhere in the world. I just chose Northern Manitoba because I know it best. Because police officers work midnights and often need a laugh, the book is a nice short sprint. I doubt that this book will end up in a lot of corporate boardrooms. I do hope that Rolicking City Police will live beside the toilet, in the cell block, in the back seat of police cars and especially at crime scenes. Please pick up the book, put your feet up and grab a good single malt scotch. Of course, if you are in the toilet, just "stand down" on the feet thing. Enjoy the book, it was written with a good time in mind!

Chapter 1
Rolicking City Police

A young cop entered Staff Sergeant Earl Jean's office. Constable Wesley was approaching four years service. Pretty much everything Wesley touched turned ugly. Some cops were like that. The other constables felt he was riding out a hex. Wesley had inhaled a dose of bad karma. He was now cursed for life. This was the consequence of his failure to punctually bleed a live chicken. When Wesley worked, everything evil happened in the city. This included but was not limited to dead bodies, fires, explosions, car accidents, train derailments and UFO sightings.

Wesley had just entered Earl's office; more aptly deemed, the inner sanctum of sanity. The old staff glared with both the disdain and amusement of a man almost two decades his senior. Wesley detailed the morning's events to his boss in a manner indicative that Earl should give a shit.

The staff sergeant surfaced back to reality when Wesley (the troops called him Bush Face) turned a sideways glance to the "looking glass window." Earl had coughed and a self propelled morsel of breaky struck the slick surface. It wasn't one of those wee bits of toast morsels but a fully fledged, shimmering, snot yellow chunk of egg yolk. Earl and Bush Face quietly acknowledged the projectile and returned to the meeting at hand.

No one really knew how the troops came up with Bush Face. Maybe it was that turned up nose, goatee or perhaps something else, most exquisitely female. Earl didn't care. Sooner or later he would cherish his own time spent with a superior. There was almost certain knowledge that his off color language would eventually catch up to him.

He would eventually have to answer to a greater subset of corporate gods, "Staff Sergeant Jeans is it true that you referred to a constable in the Rolicking City Police as a bush face?" Earl relished in his own, more highly evolved, sense of battle planning. He had his answer already formulated in his mind. Something like, "No, it was Constable F.Y. Bush Face. You strange little gangrened ferret." The canned response lived under his blotter. Beneath the blotter sheltered a multitude of cross outs and otherwise defunct phone numbers.

Earl felt a rising T3 giggle which was immediately surpassed by a festering T3 fart. There was something in those damn pills that was certainly not from this world!

Bush Face elaborated, "Staff, there was a call and we had a bad scene...."

Earl asked, "Is anyone dead?"

"No, but...!" Earl slammed down his current issue of "Tekno Hunt" magazine! A dozen sticky notes were uprooted from the desk. Bush's eyes reflected the fear of one not only green but green stupid. The boss hated green stupid. Why the hell is simple communication so damn tough for these kids?

Earl exploded, "Okay, we got zero dead and you are in my office—what's the drill?"

Bush wished that he could remove himself from this crime scene and just fade into the picture of the Queen that covered the fist hole in the wall. He continued, "Sorry Staff, by a bad scene I meant we screwed up. We simply didn't have enough troops on hand. We got called to the break and enter an hour ago. It was supposed to be over. At least that's what the complainant called in. We drove up like usual—figured it was routine."

Earl Jeans, in charge of the Rolicking City Police (RCP) had been with the Department for close to 22 years. In reality, just like any police department, the numbers of officers did not often equate to "sane boots" on the ground. Earl was in charge of everything "operational" and most things "irrational" that hit the RCP.

Earl found himself thinking about the cabin, and what he needed to buy at the hardware store. He knew it was wrong not to give an absolute shit about the crew. It just seemed that most were not worthy of anyone giving a shit. Earl wondered if their parents could have even cared. To raise a kid green stupid implied that they too, were by default, the mutant stock of inbred leprechauns.

The constable labored on. It was a painful exercise in forced communication, "There was me and another constable. We walked in the florist shop and noted that the cash drawer was still open." The owner of the shop was Val Thicket. The troops liked her a lot: she smelled damn good. As if for sensual sampling, she wore her pups out "tight and high."

Earl looked up, he was somewhat intrigued, "What was Val wearing...? Was it the tank top with the *Rolicking Lips* logo on the front?" He reflected silently to himself who cared about the back? The front, I say—the damn front! The old boss did not realize it, but he was having a significant old guy moment. Lately, he seemed to be a victim of his own spontaneous utterings. It wasn't really demonic. It was more symptomatic of a hard lined, multi tasked environment that had gone unchecked. Both the staff sergeant and the office crew were the obvious victims of his longevity.

"Hey Bush," Earl fired, "Is there an end to all this or am I going to have to call the boss in Mindless Bliss?"

Bush detailed, "Me and Jay ... the other constable, took a statement from Val. She explained that she came to the shop at 8:00 A.M. and found the till open. She left it as is and called in the incident. We checked the back door, and it was still locked. No sign at all how someone got in. The bad guy must have blazed out. We weren't sure ... but we wrote in the file that the bad guy went in the front door. He must have got out ... somehow."

Earl was clearly agitated. It's the somehow of policing that always seemed to blow back the most yolk. He asked, "So then what, you got me on edge now...?"

Bush blurted out, "Well we left with our statement in hand, went through the drive thru and then the call came."

Earl hated drive thru's worse than dumb cops. Why can't they just park the fucking car and walk in the shop? Oh, you wouldn't want that now. Talking to folks and interacting!

Bush went on, noticeably rattled and quipped up, "Do you want me to get Jay?"

A Jay and a Bush in the office at one time was just too much. A sudden calm flooded his mind, the T3 had taken an hour ago had somewhat dulled the sting of the morning. Earl said, "Just finish the damn story...!"

"Jay was driving," Bush stammered and tried to feather back a stutter, "ww, ww, wee, we were in the line and sort of boxed in. Then we got the call that someone had just run out of Val's shop. It was too late. We already paid our money at the first window and we were caught, kind of wedged in—waiting for our joe. We couldn't leave if we wanted to. We were the only ones working. Once we got our coffee, we went right back to the shop. Val was not happy at all. My guess is she'll make a complaint—sorry."

Earl hated to state the obvious, but it occurred to him that this was often his job. The staff leaned back on the city issued, leatherette bound, no expense spared command chair and fired out the seemingly obvious analysis, "The fucker was in there all along!"

Bush Face replied, "We don't know that for sure."

Earl said, "Please leave and thanks for coming in today."

Earl wondered to himself just how bad this day was going to be. Pills can't fix everything. That job was best reserved for the domain of whiskey. His fingers prayed lightly over the top of the keyboard and hovered with the presumption of intent. The digits banged slowly but with resolving impact. The intensity of force was consistent with his apprenticeship on a 1981 "Royal" typewriter. For an old guy, he considered himself pretty damn good with computers. No dueling thumbs texting like the kids, but pretty damn good. He surfed into the RCP, "Operational Procedures Manual." It used to be a hard cover manual now it was a hyperlink off the Bliss Landing District web site. The boss' intent to author meaningful and positive change was very short lived.

His Executive Assistant Gretchen, formerly known in the draconian era as, *Office Clerk* hollered, "The Mayor is on 6424!" Earl hoped that in his next life there would be some sort of silent, simpler notification system that would indicate that he had a call. It had been an issue for years, folks screaming relentlessly over the P.A. system.

"Geez ... fuck sakes," Earl muttered while conquering the "kiddy proof" pill bottle in one awkward motion. The lid was liberated. He tossed in another pill with his coffee. There was a time when one damn hit would do the trick. The pill semi-dissolved and the surface tension stuck to his palate. A primal reflex ensued. Tongue darted over moldy old palate trying not to choke. Hot coffee and pills almost never mixed. He belted back another sip of deemed, *normal coffee*—always black.

Earl dialed into 6424 and the Mayor Deb Dumas was hard out of the starting gate spewing indiscernible verbiage reminiscent of his dear old angry mom.

Earl cut off the waw, waw, waw sound with, "No good morning ... no, how ya doing?"

The Mayor or *M.D.* as most folks called her chirped up, "What is the deal with the overtime through the roof? Do you have some kind of fantasy budget that I'm not aware of...?"

Earl was clearly not in the mood for any kind of confrontation. He expected anyone in Rolicking to take firm note that he was wearing a gun. He had an innate dislike for politics. It was accepted as a necessary evil but at the same time, he openly refused to play the party line. Rolicking City was equally divided on politics. M.D. was new to the game but she came from a long line of politicians. Her father and her grandfather both served as mayor. She was often accused of being born with a silver spoon in her mouth. Her Worship was both astute and savvy enough to skirt the issue.

In many ways M.D. and Earl were too much alike. Like two moose ramming racks over a chunk of bad tundra—the battle made little sense. Earl liked to ram heads. He just wasn't in the mood that day. The staff knew it was a comic book cliché to play the hard lined cop. He had simply grown fondly into the part. He often wondered if he was really so hard lined or if, as he truly believed—the new troops were just too damn soft.

M.D. relentlessly pursued, "Earl, are you listening to me?"

Overtime was a problem. He knew the dollars of the game. However, there were some variables in policing that were inevitable. "Madam Mayor, let me clarify," Earl stated politely. Earl loved *Madam Mayor;* he thought the title befitted the bitch she truly was. Earl amplified, "Yes, we spent some bucks, but we really had no choice. Sometimes we do get the odd body around here that isn't alive. We have an obligation to explore the matter. The public seems to expect cops to investigate murders. If we didn't do that, then you wouldn't be in office much longer!"

The Mayor bellowed back, "$18,000 in one week was too much to digest!" M.D. was losing her patience, which was increasingly self-marginalized.

Earl jumped, "Do you really think I like to spend money? I would much rather enjoy the luxury of an adequately staffed police force. We are supposed to have 24 officers, but we are crippling along with 19. It simply costs bucks to bring cops back on overtime. My take—the cost of doing business."

Rolicking City simply did not have enough money to pay for both officers and overtime. She knew that there was a discrepancy between the officers on paper and working cops. Something more tangible was needed to sell to Council. M.D. finalized the discussion, "I expect an email today clearly outlining the costs incurred along with a detailed rationalization."

Much like the acceptance of the inevitable "last call," Earl heard that familiar dead phone line. He was almost ready to leave the office. He tried to make it happen. His body and mostly his head weren't in it for the office ride. It was now 11:00 A.M. and the way things were going he wanted to just go home at noon and call it square. Earl's pension wouldn't kick in for another three years. Even then, he would give up big bucks. For a full pension, he would have to endure 30 years with no chance of parole. At this point, he was prepared to do just about anything but catch politically fired missiles all day.

"Call double parked on 6420. Earl, it's for you…," crackled the raspy, cigarette flavored voice over the "P.A." Double parked meant someone had been on hold far too long. It was the cordial way of communicating the obviously implied declaration—pick up the fucking phone.

Earl replied, "Good, maybe they will just hang up." He often longed for a system like the internet providers and just simply call forward folks to New Delhi. That would certainly fix them. Yep, he pictured it now, some Sikh dealing with M.D. He would savor the ultimate call forward for his last day. The staff had a secret list of things to do, aptly referred to as, the "get even list." It would be executed, as it must, on his last day at the Department. The list was the second greatest love of his life.

Earl looked around his office, he wanted to bail. No easy feat in the office, no easy feat at all. The outside window did not open. He could not hurtle himself through it. The staff did have a small rectangular window facing the troops. He could only hope it was bulletproof. Of course, that was not very likely given the City budget. The looking glass window let everyone else look in—resistance at any rank was futile. Escape meant a planned trajectory out the door, past the clerks and on to a waiting stead.

Earl thought … fuck, at least John Dillinger had a wheel man! In the beginning, just leaving through the door seemed like a non issue to him. Now, it presented an everyday problem. He reclined slightly back and found himself squinting at the door. He could see the flickering shadows of the constables. He glanced over his right striped shoulder at the operational procedures he started to write. It could all wait, just like the email to the Mayor; it all could damn well wait. Earl liked T'3's there was never enough in the little bottle.

An opponent had to choose a sweet spot in order to make the exit move. Admittedly, the game was damn lame. At the same time, why waste time getting caught in a "yak fest" when you could slip out of Dodge under stealth? While exiting his jail cell, Earl casually commented to one of the constables, "Nice fucking shirt. Real nice, you got an ice mocha joka coffee drink down your front. Real god damned professional!"

Earl felt a little twisted and uneasy inside. He wasn't really mean. He just knew that if he promptly attacked, there would be the anticipated moment of mob silence thus creating, "slip time." His life had become an issue of creating more and more slip time. The victim of the attack was Constable Ron Fleury. Ron was but two weeks out of the academy in Winnipeg—he was 21 at best. He finished high school in the city. His advanced education in policing would likely begin and end with the RCP. Ron was one of the Department's first Aboriginal officers. He was a likeable kid who had spent the winter guarding in the cell block until a spot came open at the Academy. Ron was an excellent athlete and regularly skated with the younger cops. He liked the troops and they had taken an obvious shine to him. Although he originally hailed from the Rolicking area, he had been raised in the city. He was now, like most others his age, totally acclimatized to city life.

Ron looked back at Earl, "Sorry boss, it just happened. I'll make sure no one sees me. I'll go home and switch things up."

Earl retaliated like the combatant he truly was, "Yeah, you can switch up your shirt but you're stuck with that face!" That was it—Earl knew his comments were far too left field. The office standstill confirmed that just about everyone must have heard. Most of the employees had grown hardened to his sensory assaulting diction. Slip time, amounting to thirty seconds, seemed almost surreal. This included a sensory image which could best be described as clerks moving and talking in high definition slow motion.

While still on the move, a clerk flashed a telephone receiver in the staff's direction; the cord dangled precariously in the air. His only thought was simply, run Earl run! The old staff rounded second and passed the file room—he was almost home free. He shaved off the last corner while absorbing the lingering stink of the ladies washroom. It smelled worse than the gents—no one knew why. His knees came up high and his duty belt rattled. Earl pondered women are pigs. No they aren't—some wear tops with Rolicking Lips.

The staff never went home for lunch. It was problematic most days. It's not like he didn't get hungry. Most days it was 4:00 P.M. before he knew it. Earl wasn't fat or skinny. He was proud of the fact that he hadn't succumbed to that all too familiar "slothy cop" look. He drove by the florist … he had to make time to slide by. Earl was a firefighter at heart. That is to suggest, office flames. He knew that if he talked to Val about the botched drive thru caper, he would in turn; avoid her complaining to District. Anything, to avoid talking to that thirty something superintendent in Bliss, who just lived to please the whole god damn world.

Earl had long since given up trying to enchant most people. He got no bonus or incentive for delivering messages of pleasure. He liked being a cop but most importantly, he cherished life in the fast lane. Reality almost always never pleased both politicians and senior management. Some folks much preferred a career trapped in their own private world of delusion.

Earl engrossed himself in the bright sunlight and climbed into his Impala. He thought out loud while lighting up a smoke. Fuck, just my luck if Val changed her shirt.

The police radio echoed, "Staff…!" In mid salutation, Earl hurled the microphone. It ricocheted past the shotgun rack, past the laptop and off the dash.

The staff blurted out loud for the Impala to hear, "It's not right to be held captive most all of the time. Right, in the middle of a decent fantasy! God, that was fucking good!" He knew when he slid by second that they would snare him. *They* had taken on life which was beyond the scope of the employer. *They* represented the omniscient presence of tutelage. He reached up to his vest and killed his cell phone. He was now off safely to the home front.

This was his "safe house." The garage was boss, clerk and constable proof. It was not politician proof. He found that out once. The mayor lives right down the street. She could drive by his bow at any point. Earl thought … the bitch gets to go home for lunch every day, swell! Earl parked and strolled in to the house through the garage door.

The staff presumed his wife Judy would be home for lunch. Judy taught school, Grade 6. The school was about a mile away and most days she would slide by the house. Not today, Earl thought, maybe that was best. He would just vent and she would smile. He would vent some more and she would ask him about the status of house jobs that weren't done. Judy always asked about his day and that would force him to detail the whole fucking morning. Odd, at the same time, it still would have been nice to see her. Earl was the exception to the rule. He had been married to the same woman for 21 years. Earl knew that he had not worked on the marriage at all. If they were still together then it was because Judy liked the deal. No wait, tolerated. No, no … maybe got used to it.

In walked Earl's son Bob, age 14. As he walked in the house he hung his head while clutching his in vitro spawned cell phone. Most times it was as if the damn cell was embedded in his palm. Earl was taken aback. The kids never come home for lunch. Earl deduced that's because Dad will crank them right up. He wondered to himself—I bet they would slip him if they could. Sorry to disappoint, that's the old man's domain! Earl detested the tekkie toy environment. Most times his son and daughter were focused on some damn video game. Each kid had a computer in their room. Up the stairs they went, plummeting themselves into their passive reactive world. It wasn't totally their fault. After all, most kids are into the same toys. Earl knew he liked them too. He walked up the stairs to attempt speech with Caveman Bob. As usual, the boy had assumed the position; sprawled out on his bed with device in hand.

Earl enquired much like an umpire who had already made up his mind, "What the hell brings you home at this ungodly hour?" Earl braced himself. Anything could come at him now, not much slip space in the kid's room.

Bob looked for a brief moment but his fingers never missed a beat, "It's on the calendar Dad. All the kids are out—the teachers are figuring something out."

"So this is it. Big plans for this afternoon…?" Earl walked away. He wasn't up to getting into it with the kid. He was a solid teenage and he never spent a night in cells yet. A cop's standard of good is always extreme. Earl knew other cops that had not been so fortunate. Earl walked over to the fridge. He was assaulted by a visual barrage of "lite" this and "healthy" that.... He saw an old hoagie in the back, some visible fuzz—nothing major. He nuked it in the microwave and ate it over the sink "au natural." He stared out the kitchen window and he could see M.D. in her backyard eating her lunch in the garden gazebo. Earl reflected, it simply isn't right to hate a gazebo. It simply can't be the driving sign of sanity. He paced around the kitchen while he finished his express lunch.

After he ate, he wondered how long the hoagie had been there. As much as Earl didn't want to go back to the office, he knew that he couldn't stay home with the boy. He had to hang low, not much had changed since he was a kid. If you stayed home from school then necessarily, you could not be seen around town. He adjusted his body armor and turned his cell phone back on. He really didn't want to shut it off. It only had to matter once that it was on.

Chapter 2
Bliss Landing

Bliss Landing was sandwiched in the bottom of a rocky valley. It was about a four hour drive south from Rolicking City. Winnipeg was yet another three hour pilgrimage due south of Bliss. In quantitative terms, a driver could reasonably expect to absorb the flickering images of 2.1 million trees. Bliss Landing was the District Office for both the Rolicking City Police and the Fairford City Police. This hub type policing concept was born out of the bowels of a 1990's *Think Tank*. The report recommended the amalgamation of similar cities in order to better streamline administrative costs. What had evolved was a master empire comprising three cities. Folks often referred to the tri-empire as simply, *The Empire*. Earl much preferred the somewhat more metaphoric, "Mindless Bliss." The later handle truly suited the stark reality of its dark colon like existence. The empire was the embryo of career building initiatives that, more aptly; thrived on the creation of policing obstacles. All the big bosses worked out of Bliss Landing. There was another staff sergeant in Fairford City who represented Earl's counterpart.

Superintendent Harold Thompson, in charge of District, looked every bit as important as the role decreed. His uniform was immaculate. He had a fairly large corner office with exterior windows at intersecting corners. It was in the empire's rule book that staff sergeants and below got one window and those of superiority got two. Ironically, there was nothing remarkable to view out any of the panes. Harold cherished the idea of having one more window than any other police manager in the district. After all, success in life was more aptly judged by the bobbles of auspicious display.

Bobbi Pichot the clerk for District, walked into Harold's office, "The Mayor from Rolicking is on line one!" There was no P.A. system in District. This was inscribed on the goat skin parchment decree that had been laid out decades prior. Clerks were expected to physically inform their supervisors that a phone call was waiting. No one really knew what linked business process to personal etiquette. An invasive P.A. system, would simply not, have been tolerated. There were, quite apparently; no loud noises ending recess in District.

Harold accepting his fate muttered, "Great." He picked up the phone, "Hello Your Worship."

M.D. snapped, "Drop it Harold. I'm not calling because I want to." She elaborated with all the distinction associated with her political moniker, "I called Earl this morning and asked him for a run down on his overtime for the murder. Is it just too much to ask for something tangible when we spend $18,000 in a week?"

Harold made no effort to hide his disdain for the staff sergeant. He seized every opportunity to publically roast him. Harold tried to clarify, "Did you ask him for something?"

M.D. replied, "Yes, I asked him to give me something in writing clarifying, and further justifying, the costs of the investigation. I mean, we can't be spending $18,000 dollars every time someone drops dead!"

Harold thought to himself, $18,000 per body really is—damn cheap. Instead, he embraced the political machine as he knew it should be coddled, "This is unacceptable. Let me look into it and I'll get you some answers." Harold pushed the hand's free button and called Bobbi, "Would you please contact Staff Jeans and tell him that I need to see him tomorrow. I'm not sure what I have on the go, whatever works...."

Bobbi replied, "Yes Sir."

Harold quipped back, "Wait a minute, make sure we don't meet at ten or three—never at coffee time." The corporate protocol necessitated that Bobbi always refer to Harold as *Sir*. Harold loved the formality of protocol. Order and respect for one's superiors fostered a more highly evolved sense of corporate ownership and culture.

Harold scanned his emails, mostly budget items and financial forecasting. There were several items relative to the upcoming "United Police Senior Manager's Conference." It was held in the region every year just before Christmas. Someday Harold thought, I'll chair the event but first I'll have to change the damn name. Almost no one referred to the conference by its official name. It was simply reduced to a detestable acronym, "UPSM." Harold had risen up through the ranks in the fast lane. He had a Master's Degree in Political Science. After a brief competition, the City of Bliss Landing had selected him for the job. He had virtually no policing experience. Harold always argued that he had an "enforcement background." True, he worked for a brief time with the Feds in Ottawa. The position did not work out professionally. However, he did benefit from the endowment of private French language training. In terms of his current role, he was fully prepared to back up his *hello* with an audibly awkward and totally Anglo, *bonjour*.

The superintendent was of the mindset that police experience was not absolutely essential in order to effectively manage a police force. The logic was solidified in Harold's mind. You didn't need to know how to sing to produce good records. You didn't need to know how to change oil to run a garage. On that one, Harold gazed out the smaller of his two windows and reflected—he wasn't quite sure. Certainly, one could argue, that any reasonable man, would expect a garage keeper to have some general knowledge of an oil filter. He removed his glasses and rubbed his eyes. He intertwined his fingers and held his hands together—policing was no oil filter.

The issue of sound management was one firmly rooted in inspirational leadership. The Bliss Landing management style was founded on the teachings of Dr. Jake Shelby. Corporate structure was only as strong as the "rebar" that ties in the frame to the foundation. Harold had a plaque on the wall with the customary five inch piece of rebar. The steel icon was bestowed upon him by Dr. Shelby at the last UPSM Conference. It wasn't his only piece of rebar. He traveled with another length during any business travel. He had diligently learned to pack the bar in his checked luggage after its predecessor's tragic seizure at Vancouver Airport.

The five inch piece of rebar represented the five walls of corporate strength namely, personal goals, spiritual channeling, financial accountability, corporate credibility and business solidarity. There was yet another, "just in case" rebar enshrined in his right upper most desk drawer. The superintendent often clutched it tightly during conference calls. Dr. Shelby's teachings demanded that the convert reflect deeply into the rebar for five minutes, four times daily. This was not a passive action it was firmly grounded in spiritual intent. One could not simply look at the rebar. You had to reflect deeply and believe in the channeling of the bar. This was a religious exercise that demonstrated personal commitment to a corporate vision. It was the very source of a much deeper Zen inspired reflection. It angered Harold that he could never get the rebar perfectly clean. There were all those little ridges in the steel. Those damn ridges attracted and cultivated ugly brown rust all the time.

Harold was lost in the moment and knocked over his red plastic model of a 67' Corvette. The plastic chauffeur rolled tragically out of the convertible and plummeted to the floor. Harold took off his blue serge and gradually crept down to the carpet. Under the desk and in front of his chair, the "wee" impeccably dressed driver appeared to smirk back at Harold. Helplessly, the little man remained horizontally spread eagled behind a circular tuft of dust. The superintendent reached out and stretched his arm further. Eking out yet more inches, he grasped the wayward rogue. Harold loved classic cars as much as he liked the formalities of, *Sir*. He got up, brushed himself off and placed the driver gently back into his rightful position.

Glancing up to the left and beside the largest window he took note of his very well endowed "me wall." Harold thought to himself, most breathtaking. The certificates were housed in simple yet corporately elegant, black frames. The stand out certificate was the one that decreed formal rank and title. This one had classical gold leaf motif completely surrounding the document's edge. In his own mind, Harold believed he had reached an elevated level of excellence. He opened the right desk drawer and removed a tube of hand lotion. His hands were full of rebar rust—they hurt like hell.

Chapter 3
Promotions and Things

Earl walked back into the office. The headache was diminishing; it was now 1:30 P.M. He looked over at the clerk's desk. He knew they took note of every fucking second. To give that much of a shit about Earl, they must truly have disproportioned lives. Earl took a different route to his office and swung around the northwest corner. This path paralleled the "Intensive Crime Unit" (ICU). In reality, this was the "Plain Clothes Unit" (PCU). There was only one cop working. Pretty Boy (P.B.) was busy banging away on his computer. In reality, he was not that pretty but compared to guys called Bush Face, he made the "higher end" RCP cut. Earl figured he was gay. He just had that extra "X" chromosome thing about him. He heard all these rumors about the girls but there was never any evidence. P.B. had about seven years of service with the Department. He was cruising everywhere fast in his own mind.

Earl understood the reality of today's youth. They were full of grandeur and hope which almost always, exceeded their cognitive abilities. P.B. wrote the Sergeant's Exam last year but missed it by two points. It really didn't matter how much you missed it by—no promotion. No promotion, then no hope of ever working District in Bliss. Of course, there were exceptions to every promotional system. Superintendent Thompson could directly anoint under the provisions invested in the "Field Demonstrated Abilities Model" (FDAM). Essentially, this management prerogative created a situation where

14

a candidate could fail an exam but still be deemed promotable. There was currently an opening in Bliss for a sergeant position. Harold had canvassed all the eligible candidates. No one meeting the exam cut was deemed "suitable" for the position. The staffing action would now proceed via FDAM. Earl tried to give a shit. It was hard but P.B. was deemed meritorious of the staff's prodigious, *not a bad guy*. Earl sauntered into ICU and casually fired out a, "Howz it going?"

P.B replied, "Great, I'm working on my promotional docs. I was just going to print them for you so you could comment."

Earl felt his stomach turn. He was quite certain that his eyes did a 360 degree flip into his head. The staff could not help himself, "You know we have a guy out there doing break in's. We could be tossing a few assholes out there." Earl looked at P.B. poised like a little squirrel at a feeding station. He thought to himself, fuck the guy has his hands and fingers twisted like a bug.

Out came the choice words, "Staff, I'm on it … just waiting for a source to call it in."

Earl wondered, who were these mysterious people that ICU worked. The RCP paid out a fair bit of change for information. Drugs were, after all, the sexy crime of 2009. Earl knew that a break in to a flower shop was not the stuff of promotional grandeur. He further pondered that, even if it was solved, it would never make the distinction of inclusion on a "Self Vindication" form. The Self Vindication process was essentially a self appraisal system derived from actualized police examples.

In a sense, it was not the fault of the cops competing for the various promotions. It was the fault of the god's in Bliss who had decreed the masturbatory process to be the very basis for advancement. This necessarily put the hardened or not so hardened street cop to the "Shakespearian Test." To vindicate, or not to vindicate, Earl was lost in the anal platitude of the game.

The staff often wondered if the private sector operated on such a benign premise. Earl knew that he too, was a target. P.B. was competing for promotion so Earl would not only have to read the slop, but inject supervisory comments. The Vindication had to be submitted on hard copy and duly signed. It could easily trash a whole day. Earl knew, deep down, that he did not want to lose P.B. There was simply no one else in the Department that could fill his spot. In the big picture, he was user friendly and relatively hard working. As if the stars were seemingly in line, he would actually pick up the phone when called to duty. Earl knew that the sergeant job that P.B. was competing for fell under Harold Thompson. If P.B. ever got in that job, he would certainly end up jumping out of one of the two hallowed windows. In a glass half full analysis, the staff surmised, well at least it wouldn't be a Rolicking file.

There were only three officers in PCU and it was headed up by Detective Kate O'Malley. Earl liked Kate. She had been around the RCP for nearly as long as Earl. She had never married and had no kids. Five years ago, she came out of the closet and was now fully patched gay. He had known some of her partners over the years. Kate was not like most chick cops. She was tempered, never moody or down in the dumps. In fact, most of the time she was just as quick with a head shot to the psyche as Earl was to the groin. Earl jabbered up, "Kate, you out solving B & E's?"

Kate replied, "No, that's your job to police the drive thru."

Set and serve, Earl knew that he had taken a well executed shot. It was delivered by one of the best. P.B. just stared on while leaving more of a "bug like" impression by the minute. Earl thought to himself, just how fucking lucky he will be to read the Vindication. He knew that Rolicking wasn't exactly the hot bed of intrigue yet he knew things would read way, way up and beyond.

It was now almost 3:00 P.M. Earl always corralled someone to partake in coffee. Yes, it was a civilized ritual beckoning back to another era of policing. Coffee in the office, fancy that…. We would sit and talk, while collectively brow beating those not in the room. Earl could remember back to his formative years when everything stopped mid afternoon. There used to be a T.V. in the back room aptly called the coffee room—sadly it was no more. Now, whoever dreamed up the previously inviting "coffee room" would never be able to envision its current, board like transition.

Offered up for scrutiny, one could find tea, hot chocolate and even some of that damn pouch soup. There was also a smattering of dehydrated noodle packets! Food that grew under the duress of boiling water was not—normal food. Food that grew upon the addition of any fluid was more appropriately aligned with "sea monkeys." Earl kept a secret stash of coffee along with some emergency pills. It was fail safe. If they found that stash, there was yet an extra coffee can in his downstairs locker.

Earl walked in the coffee room. Bush and Jay were already positioned around the table. Bush was eating some "leafy material" out of a plastic container. Earl could not get over how new cops brought their *home food* to work in plastic dishes. Home food should stay at home. Work food, Earl thought for a minute, well—we should go out. Plastic lunches simply never happened 20 years ago.

Earl held himself back from any further culinary analysis, "Hi boys, whatz shaking?" The old staff was famous for his, whatz shaking? Earl noticed that each officer had a cell phone flipped open and ready on the table. They were eating, talking, drinking, and sending text messages. Earl was very pleased with himself for knowing about text messages. It came out of a greater need, largely cultivated at home, to try and relate to kids. He would never understand the need to be so connected. It was the very thing that he despised most about the job. Although, he had zero tolerance for text, he did get the odd message from the crew. They would often, while on the road, field this question or that problem. They would text him something and most times he would just call them back.

He remembered a message he got last week from Bush, "Made a rest, fite, need help." Isn't that what the damn radios are for...? You can fight and text at the same time, bonus! Of course, valor necessarily dictates, that if you get the worse of it, you wouldn't want the whole world to know! Text in the final analysis, could not be avoided anywhere. It was a medium of communication that was now firmly embedded in the annals of policing.

Earl rummaged through the cupboard and looked for his mug. He saw it was dirty and sitting upside down in the sink. Sacrilege, Earl grimaced, holding out his hands while steadying himself in the galley. Worst yet, there appeared to be chocolate residue along the rim. Earl grabbed another clean mug. It had the Bliss Landing District logo on it, coat of arms or something. It looked more like a seal holding an octopus. Wait; let's dim the lights ... possibly something much more provocative!

There was that awkward silence, Earl liked it. Any time the rank and file was in the midst of a discussion, he would walk in the room and invade their space. Earl executed the room invasion better than any gang member. Almost to say, "Hi, I am here. Sorry about your damn luck but I am here anyway!" The young coppers kept texting. Earl figured those bastards are cyber whispering about me. Ten years ago, they would have been forced to verbalize. Now—he reached back, I think I'm getting thumb fucked.

Earl found himself noticeably awkward clutching the Bliss Landing District mug. He put it down and suddenly realized that he did not really want to be around these kids. He started to leave when Gretchen met him at the doorway.

Gretchen said, "You got an email. The boss wants to see you in Bliss." She elaborated, "Don't read it ... it will just piss you off. They want to see you tomorrow at 2:00 P.M. with a financial update for the murder."

Earl walked into his office, he noticed an envelope, *Personal and Confidential* was checked off in bold. He stared at it like a hooker on her first date and then picked it up. He noticed that someone had taken the time to tape up the ends. Earl wondered to himself why anyone would go to such an extent to protect something so blatantly insignificant. He remained transfixed on the envelope and said out loud for no one to hear, "I know, I know because it's something terribly important about them!" On that note, Earl reflected, now let's go and do something important for Earl.

Earl pulled up to Val's shop with the unmarked 2005 dark blue Impala. He first adopted the old Impala after District did a workplace hazard study. The study arrived at the conclusion that it was unsafe for two officers to ride in it at the same time. This was because there were a lot of things in the Impala namely a shotgun rack, computer, radio, ticket holder, flashlight holder, a double dipped donut, GPS and two steel coffee mugs. In reality, the exercise was part and parcel of a workplace initiative fueled by the "District Health and Wellness Association."

The Impala, so the study concluded, could not safely hold all the equipment and two police passengers. Even without one of the coffee cups, crash tests conclusively proved that the passenger would be at dire risk from flying debris. Earl shook his head. The lingering tangible issue was that the Department still owned at least four of these vehicles. Under the current vehicle management plan, it wasn't as if you could just go and trade them in. So bit by bit they were left for the plundering of bosses everywhere. This "beaute" was the only one left. The others had been plundered by District. Earl loved the Impala. It was skinned with the scuffs and tears from years of abuse. There was that "je ne sais quoi" which equated to the collective scent of dated puke and moldy sunflower seeds. Much like Earl, this vehicle evoked history.

The flower shop was situated in a busy strip mall. It was very difficult to park. Earl dug out his "Police Officer on Duty" sign and fired it on the dash. He then rolled into the handicap parking. Earl knew, this would make the Impala a target for all … little did they know—he had the mighty card of exclusion. Earl walked into the shop. The little bell above the door rang out his arrival. Val was at the cash waiting on Daryl Marley. Daryl was not Jamaican. He was of Irish descent….

Earl asked, "Daryl, someone's birthday?" He then tacked on, "Hope nobody died?" As soon as Earl uttered the words, he knew he was totally "limbed out." Zero slip space and Val glared right back at him. Earl was not a tactical guy by any means. It was apparent that he had minimal options for strategic repositioning. The customer must have sensed something. He had known Earl for decades.

Daryl replied while exiting the store, "No sweat Earl, he'd been dying for a long time anyway."

Val was quick at bat and commented, "Another one of Rolicking's finest! At least this time the cop saw the guy leave!"

The old staff leaned on the counter, "Val, I know today has sucked. It can only get better, a dozen roses please." She had the tank top on. Earl found himself staring at Val below the neck line. The logo on the tank top looked even more inspiring with the eyeball zoom. It was totally unprofessional (the rule book would say so) but right now, it mattered not.

Val clarified, "White or Red?"

For a minute Earl thought they were talking wine or something. Most times he only bought flowers when he was in trouble. Even then, it was always the "ones on sale." Earl had an uncanny knack of initiating an act of distinction followed by a pulverizing emotional blow to the head.

Earl blurted out, "It doesn't matter they all die the same." While Val wrapped up the flowers, Earl shifted his weight awkwardly while focusing out the street window.

The staff said, "Val thanks very much. I just wanted to come by and tell you personally that we will get the guy that did the break in."

Val replied, "It's not the crime it's more the attitude of your guys. Hey, I know my shop is nothing. I know it wasn't a bank robbery or a homicide but it's my shop just the same!"

Earl asked, "Do you mind if I look around?" Earl liked doing personal "look arounds" at crime scenes. In the old days you brought in the forensic guys, seized stuff that didn't matter and called in the dog. You did it simply because it was part of "the police show." Even if the cops didn't catch the bad guy, the victims enjoyed the effort. Police work is not only about solving crime. It's about the illusion of giving a shit. Whether he cared or not, the illusion was absolutely key. It was the illusion that left folks with a good taste in their mouth. Earl often thought, it was the greater sense of presentation that new cops lacked. There was far too much effort placed on business process and not enough on flair.

Earl took a look at the back door. There was stock piled up high against the door. Earl commented, "How long has this stuff been here?"

Val clarified, "For over a year. The Fire Chief has been bugging me to clear it out."

Earl continued, "Is there any other way in or out of the store?"

Val losing her patience, "Well you could just beam yourself in here but most folks prefer the front door."

Earl asked, "And this morning, how did the bad guy leave?"

Val let out a breath, "Do you guys not communicate with each other? One of your guys was over here about three hours ago. I gave him a statement. Here, he gave me his card. The card read Constable Peter Bolan, AKA by friends and foe alike as, P.B. At the same time, Earl noticed a jiggle and the Rolicking Lips logo seemed to pucker up.

Val elaborated, "He went out the damn front door."

Earl said, "Someone went out the front door but we really don't know who." The staff had no plans to buy flowers. It wasn't anyone's birthday. He sure didn't want Judy to get the wrong idea that he had done something bad.

This was especially true with a road trip to Bliss planned the next day. It wasn't normal for Earl to panic—simply not his nature.

He gave the flowers to Val and said, "Thank you." Earl did a 180 degree turn and left the store. It would temporarily appear that he survived the handicap parking caper.

Earl went 10-8 "back in service" on the police radio. It then occurred to him that he had forgotten to go 10-7 "out of service." Earl deliberated as he pulled of the driveway, I wonder if Val would tell anyone that he just gave her flowers. Damn, he had not covered himself off. The error represented a distinct failure to maintain adequate slip space. Earl was livid. "Of course," Earl rationalized out loud, "it's no big deal to Val 'cause she hangs with flowers all day."

Chapter 4
The Cop Shop

It was now 4:15 P.M. and Earl wanted to do one quick thing before he left. He had to be able to tell the superintendent in Bliss that he sent the Mayor "something." There was no time to grab up all the overtime sheets and shift schedules and figure out where the $18,000 went. Earl inserted his trusted encryption token into the computer. He stared out his looking glass window and most of the constables were on the road. No constables, then no problems. The computer surfaced to life and the staff surfed into his email. Nothing but captions in red everywhere, *Urgent, Urgent* carved on the subject lines. Earl never responded quickly to anything urgent. In his mind, if someone had the audacity in this day and age to think that double urgents would garner his attention—they were sadly mistaken. He couldn't even open some emails because the system would track that a given message had been opened. Earl glowered at the sea of red. There was one, a single non-highlighted email tossed in the cyber gloom. Oddly, it stood right out because someone decent had sent it, Kate O'Malley. The email read simply;

Had P.B. attend Val's shop and take a more detailed statement than the first crew. It's sitting in an envelope on your desk. Heard you were going to Bliss tomorrow. Can I tag along? I have a statement to take in Hill Mountain.

This was the first "e-blurb" of good news in awhile. It was actually double good news because there was nothing truly evil in the envelope like a self Vindication. Earl poked his head out of his office and looked both ways like he was five years old, all clear.

Gretchen was still pounding the keyboard. She commented, "Trying to sneak outta here?"

Earl while still on the move, "You got that right...." He rounded first, then second and saw Kate in ICU. Earl leaned on the door. He realized he was out of breath; that sucked, "Hey, thanks for the statement and no problem tagging along if you can live with the Impala and a little cigarette smoke." Hill Mountain was a small community about half way to Bliss. The only good thing about going to Bliss was the fact that Earl could stop by the cabin. Earl said, "I have to be there at 2:00 P.M. so can we leave at 7:00 A.M.?"

Kate blurted out, "Why so damn early?"

Earl clarified, "Because no one is around here at 7:00 A.M. and we can bail with no probs."

Kate said, "You are about the most transparent man I know. Okay, early but we hit the drive thru and you are buying."

At the same moment, Earl realized he didn't send the email to M.D. Earl often found if he was juggling too much at once, the obvious would be the first thing to forget. Earl re-rounded second.

Gretchen did not even bat an eye and kept typing, "I sent you a zinger. Remember, the Mayor?"

Earl did not reply. He spun around feet up in his chair and opened up his email. He typed;

Good Afternoon Madam Mayor,
Further to our discussion this morning, I would like to thank you for your patience in the matter. In order to clarify the overtime issues for the most recent homicide, I will have to verify all claims relative to the tasking completed by our Plain Clothes Unit. I cannot further elaborate on this issue until such time that I complete this audit function. I regret that I will be on the road tomorrow. If this is an urgent matter, please contact Detective Kate O'Malley.
Have a good night!
Earl....

The staff specialized in correspondence that clarified absolutely nothing.

There was after all, great depth in stating squat. He thought to himself, no one can say that I did not respond. Of course the superintendent would expect to be copied but Earl would just say he forgot. If he got backed in the corner by the boss he would simply ask Gretchen to forward the email. To complete the cover story, he would brief Kate the next day. She would be so advised that the tag along to Bliss was last minute stuff. Cops were also good students. Earl had certainly absorbed much learning over the years. Covering off your "mistruths" was deemed a cherished passion to most cops. Most husbands learn to lie very well. Husbands that are police supervisors have indeed, mastered the art of deceptive embellishment.

Earl didn't even take the time to say good night to Gretchen. In a classic avoidance from the normal routine, Earl walked right out the front door of the Department. The front desk clerks would never expect this move. Earl knew he had to save this exit routine and use it very sparingly. He walked around to the parking lot and got in his 1992 Ford pickup truck. It was sky blue with a torn white stripe decal on the driver's side. The truck was totally "Earl." It even had the rifle rack on the rear window which now hung empty. Earl lamented the days when he could drive around with the .308 in the rack. Damn gun laws, they were never intended for cops. Now, he just stuffed the rifle in back of the driver's seat. Folks should damn well realize that I have a gun.

Earl took the long way home around the southern loop. Rolicking City had seen better times. There were quite a few shops with "closed" signs dangling in their windows. The Northern Manitoba mining community of Rolicking City was but 8200 people back in 1981. Now, it was closer to 13,000. A national big box store had moved into town which put some major economic pressure on the small family business. Earl didn't mind because the prices in the North had never been so good. There were even a few new restaurants in town. Ever since "Mushroom Pizza" had come to Rolicking things were looking up. As long as you were content to eat the same stuff all the time, you would never miss the "haute cuisine" of the big city. He drove by the hardware store. He wanted to fly in there and get some bolts for the cabin. Earl was always tinkering at the cabin. When the kids were young they went with him all the time. Now both were teenagers accompanied with social complexities that chained them to the city.

Heaven forbid you go to the woods for a couple of days. Cell phones did not work at the cabin. No text, no life … how come Darwin never came up with this? Parking was always tight at the hardware store. Earl reached down out of instinct for his "Police Officer on Duty" sign and then he realized he was in his own truck. He parked on the street and down a bit further from the presumed, target zone. It was a still a no parking zone but all the cops knew Earl's truck. If he got a ticket, he wouldn't pay it anyway. If he didn't pay, he would just receive a snotty email from the City, then a formal letter chaser and finally that would be it. Earl pondered, what is the point of having parking By-Laws that merely wield an email hammer?

The staff walked into the hardware store and he said, "Hi" to Jean Simmons who worked the cash. Jean had her arm in a sling but she still managed to work. Earl could not help but think of the pile of off duty doctor notes that he had on his desk. Earl had only been sick three times in his 22 years. Well really, he had been sick more often but he only missed three days of work. There was a sort of inherent pride in simply coming into work when you were dead.

In the old days, Rolicking cops never called in sick. You simply would not have wanted the confrontation with your boss and most importantly, the ridicule from your peers. Now it was, more or less, a badge of honor to take every single benefit afforded by the organization. This included but was not limited to mat leave, pat leave, marriage counseling, fertility counseling, partner counseling, sensitivity counseling, partner assistance programs, next of kin bereavement leave, birth of child leave, sex change modification leave and of course, loony leave.

No one could ever talk about loony leave. It was referred more aptly by the powers in Bliss as "Medical Leave." On the floor, the troops simply referred it as "LL." There was no fooling the cops on the floor. They would perceive every single deceptive move. The constables were very well versed in the same poem. In theory, there was a corporate code for medical leave. This code was to be fully documented on the shift schedules. The Watch Commanders would instead, simply write, "LL." Let's face it; in any small town it was impossible to cloak reality. Earl's thoughts ponged from ear to ear as he glanced over the myriad of nuts and bolts. He was looking for two eight inch cement anchor bolts. The hardware store was a flashback to his childhood. Little brown bags hung in the top tray of a grey layered, turn style type carrousel. The fastener carousal consisted of 12 layered stages and comprised a total of 78 bins. The choice was always left to the customer. You could buy 2, 3, or 63 bolts. It was remarkable; a vendor that didn't drive the customer to a predetermined, quantity neutral, blister pack.

The only trouble was, at any given time, Earl always needed a bolt that was on the lower shelf. Maybe they moved the hardware around. Earl wasn't sure. It didn't matter if he needed a nut, bolt or a washer—the product was always near the floor. This meant crawling down in the prone position and dredging up the stock number. One you found the damn number then "old guy eyes" took over. Sure, the number was there but it was printed in god damned "4 font." Heaven forbid you get to the till without the dreaded magic number. Earl was still in uniform and represented an opposing force.

There was no hip hop in Earl but he got down and dirty. He squinted, removed his glasses and deciphered the skew number. From the floor, Earl glanced up to the ceiling and he could see a pad of paper near the top self. Fuck it—he wrote the number on his hand. The old staff was way past caring about personal perception. Rolicking's finest sprawled out in the hardware store posed no insult to either his vanity or professional reputation. Earl still felt a little weird not caring any more about the toe shine on the boots. There was a time when he gave a shit about the uniform now it was more of an overly restrictive annoyance. Earl clutched the bolts and got up to his feet while simultaneously fighting off a case of the dizzies. The only brown bag left was a giant one. He shrugged and declined it out of size and not as the "enviro-friendly" guy he could never be. He sauntered up to the cash while perusing the sale items in the main aisle.

Earl enquired, "Jean you are hurting. What happened?" Earl had known Jean for most of his "cop life." Jean's husband Barry died in the big mining accident of '87. It was Earl who gave Jean the Next of Kin (NOK) notification. Earl was very junior at the time. To this day there existed a strange affinity between the two.

Jean not to be outdone by Earl blurted, "Me fell down some stairs." Jean was originally from Newfoundland.

Earl now looking very dusty commented, "Really and you can work the cash with one wing."

Jean replied, "No choice, the bills come either way." Earl loved the simplicity of Jean's logic. It was the financial inevitability of bills that spurred a simple decision to come to work. He doubted very much that the hardware store had "LL."

Jean piped up, "Bin number." Earl showed Jean his hand. Despite Jean's attempt, his flesh would not scan. Jean meticulously entered the numbers off Earl's hand and still no luck. Life literally hung in the balance until the price was tallied. This was one of the staff's biggest fears. To assume the prone position again—was simply too much like work.

Jean aggressively evaluated the situation. With the common sense resolve of an islander, she piped up, "They look like 49 cent anchors. Here we go … that'll be $1.18 with tax.

Earl loved the fact that he could buy bolts so cheap—less than a coffee actually. On the way out he grabbed a bag of free popcorn. He walked across to his truck. He thought to himself, no parking ticket—absolute bonus! He didn't really care one way or the other. It simply was one less email from the City. Some days Earl was in a rush to get home but today would not be one of those days.

It was now around 5:00 P.M. Earl knew that Judy would likely be home. Once Earl walked in the front door he knew that slip space would be impossible. Before you actually go home, it was critical that you pick off as many errands as you can. Earl looked up in the cab of the pickup and lit a smoke. Once lit, he had to finish his butt—there was a commitment.

He cruised by the extreme south end of town. The highway heading to Bliss beckoned him. Well, to be honest, it was more a cabin call. Earl coughed as he smoked. Out of reflex he coughed into his hand while attempting to bend his elbow. Melanie insisted that he cough into his the crux of his elbow. The old staff knew he would someday master said crux. He was now at the stage in life where conditioned motor movement often trumped bowel movement. Coughing into an elbow simply involved far too much tactical thought. He never used to cough so much. Of course, he was never accustomed to crawling around a hardware store floor.

Maybe, it was the popcorn and smoke combo. The old staff really wanted to have a beer in his lap to properly complete the picture. Earl almost never wore his uniform home. In the old days, when the kids were young he made sure he locked his gun up in the office. It was today's spontaneous exit out the front door of the Department that forced him off side. Earl hated being off his game. Good operational balance was something to be sought after. He never considered himself a "Philippe Petit" on the tight rope. Certainly, Cirque de Rolicking would never call.

In a social context, Earl also demanded balance. He demanded balance in the office and strived for it at home. Balance in conjunction with defined principles, Earl pondered—was something not easily obtained in life. Earl noted M.D.'s vehicle in his rearview mirror. It was odd. The well endowed air freshener dangling from the rearview mirror seemed to warn him. The pine forest scent was long gone. Only the beauty of the silhouette cardboard figure lived on. M.D. would naturally turn onto Earl's street right behind him. If they met, there would be an awkward social collision followed by the obligatory political joist. Fuck that! Earl recoiled and signaled an abrupt turn to the extreme right.

It was a tight and very well executed move. Earl looked through the rearview mirror and saw his adversary's Saab turn into her driveway. He questioned how anyhow can drive a car with two adjoining vowels? The air freshener girl nodded in agreement as she bounced proudly on the flimsy yellow string. The air fresheners pine tree background was ridiculously overshadowed by her obvious assets.

Earl was all good to go now. He just had to wait about ten minutes. It was late summer and M.D. always took the time to check out her damn flower beds. Earl knew she looked at his flowers and plants in disgust. This was the staff's single most important reason for not giving a shit about the flower bed. He went out of his way to ensure that his gardening looked ugly as hell. Let's face it; nothing Earl spawned was ever going to feel right to M.D.

Chapter 5
The Home Front

Earl parked his truck beside Judy's car. He finished his smoke and went into his house through the garage. He could hear voices in the basement. He went upstairs to the bedroom to get out of his "monkey suit." Earl used to be in Kate's job about five years ago. He liked the plain clothes gig. The monkey suit simply never fit right—it was built for maximum discomfort. It was as if there was some guy in the "Bliss Uniform Standards Division," who informed someone that truly fucking mattered, "Honest Sir, they have tons of room on their duty belts. We can easily fit more shit."

Earl looked down at his duty belt. He actually had more toys and things on it then a super hero! He had his issue 9 mm, handcuff pouch, first aid mask, pepper spray, portable radio holder, expandable baton, and bullet clips. There were also a flashlight and holder.

Flashlights were an article of kit that had no standard. The issued flashlights were yellow and looked like they came from a toy factory. Over the years Earl had seen many of the yellow flashlights shatter over a culprit's head. Typically, either end of the flashlight would explode under the impact subsequently hurdling "d cell" batteries into the street. There were probably lots of guys in prison with bits of bright yellow plastic embedded in their scalps. All the cops now bought their personal flashlight of choice. There were cops with blue lights, yellow lights and strobe lights. Strobe lights were supposed to immobilize criminals in much the same manner as 50,000 volts up the ass. Earl still loved the big black "Maglite." It proudly displayed dings all over the surface. Hookers notched bed posts and cops notched flashlights.

Earl often wondered how the chick cops managed all the gear. As soon as Earl thought it, he repositioned himself and repeated the politically acceptable terminology. He looked into the mirror and said out loud, "No Earl, persons of small stature."

That was the correct terminology and in reality, it was bang on. There were probably smaller guys on the RCP than girls. Earl had to really watch comments like that around Judy. She would take a comment like that and attach some sort of pre-Cambrian reference to it.

Earl could hear her now, "So are you saying that women on the RCP are fatter than the guys?" The next step is a given, "So you must think that I am fat, is that it...?" In reality, Earl thought nothing of the fact or fat. Judy always dressed nice for school and around town. The old cop/husband really didn't care if Judy packed on any weight. Of course, there goes another potential comment to spur on the wee beastie.

Earl locked up his gun. He knew this was dumb. The kids were old enough now but he did it anyway. In the old days, revolvers more aptly called "chunks" were mostly hidden in freezers—right beside the whiskey bottle. If you got called out in the night, it might be a cold chunk but you sure weren't fumbling with combinations or looking for keys. Keys for any gun were necessarily left in a more vulnerable place. Earl had tried hiding them, but invariably he could not remember where he put them. Most cops he knew kept the gun keys in a desk drawer. With the introduction of the 9 mm ten years ago came about a much more rigid application of safety protocol. The staff reached into his dresser drawer and pulled out his favorite T shirt which read, "Cops Rock and Bad Guys Suck." Like he had exchanged recent gun fire with a desperado, there were fake bullet holes all over the shirt.

Earl walked downstairs and he rounded the home game version of second. In Earl's world the office and the house were segregated according to sporting lingo. It didn't matter that the words came from different sports—it was the implication of the sentiment. The goal was the bed, second was the dining room, third was the fridge and of course home plate was the bar. Earl stopped at home plate and grabbed a hexagonally shaped rocks glass. He poured an Earl sized shot of neat, always single malt, scotch. In a sense, home plate and the goal were somewhat linked together. In Earl's mind, there still remained that geographic distancing between the main floor and the upstairs.

Judy didn't like it when Earl had a drink before supper. Of course, she was also smart enough to try and hide any negativity. Judy was still dressed in her school garb. She sported professional looking attire with a smart white blouse and black pants. She also had a purple scarf thingy draped around her neck. Earl looked on, scotch in hand. He gazed intently at the scarf that haphazardly dangled above the food prep.

Judy enquired, "How was your day?"

Earl replied almost of habit, "Same old." Now that was truly conditioned behavior! Bob was on the couch with joy stick in hand. Earl's 15 year old daughter Melanie "apparently" represented the multiple voices in the basement. The old staff savored the whiskey and felt somewhat compelled to force the banter with the missus. The single malt scotch etched a happy and penchant burn down his throat. Earl thought to himself, that he was far better off to spin out some trivial conversation then, wait for confrontation. Better some idle chit chat then sit and wait for the dreaded booze shot!

Earl enquired in a trumped up and seemingly caring manner, "How was Grade 6 today—flunk anyone?" Judy continued to cut carrots. Earl noticed that when he spoke, she cut down harder on the board. Highly trained cop that he represented led him to believe that this was not simply coincidence.

Judy replied, "We don't flunk anyone anymore. You should know that by now!" Earl knew this situation was going nowhere fast. In fact, there was a greater risk in remaining in the kitchen. There was a sweet spot between second and home plate where Earl could actually see the boy. He knew conversation with the teenager would be impossible. He had been "cybertized." Earl knew this look, it was a bad one. He had entered a deep, deep trance from power gaming all afternoon. Earl was positive that if he flung a copy of "Buck Azz'ed" beside the kid he'd still remain transfixed to the tube.

In the entire world, there was one person who Earl always had time for, it was his daughter Melanie. The young lady was like her dad in so many ways. In other, more refined aspects; she was the spitting image of her mom. Very creative, she loved singing and music. When she was younger they had tried music lessons. Melanie banged on the piano more out of a sense of parental obligation than intrinsic love to make music. Lately, she had started to take voice lessons. She would cloister herself in the basement and practice her tunes. Earl bought her a second hand karaoke machine. It was so old that it came with cassettes and not DVD's. There were no wireless microphones in the 80's; a six foot umbilical cord firmly anchored the dancer to song.

* * * *

Melanie didn't like it when Dad spontaneously intruded on her private world of voices. Dad always announced himself while descending down the stairs. It was a vision accompanied with precise sequencing that Melanie had grown up with. Initially, the royal decree sounded which self proclaimed his imminent arrival. Finally, the parental apparition materialized around her—its fingers tightly clutching the single malt. She never witnessed her dad fall down the stairs. He was most certainly overdue. Dad sure didn't have either the cadence or motility of his younger days. She liked the fact that her dad was upfront about things. Most times she didn't have to wonder what he thought. Their relationship was much easier on the psyche than the convoluted mind games with Mom.

Her old man didn't stink but Melanie always knew when he was in proximity. There was that fine line that odor drew between stink and scent. Melanie thought, scotch and cigarettes fall somewhere in between. It's funny how one person's scent can be another person's stink. Fancy that, there had actually been complaints in the school from smokers that objected to perfume and cologne.

* * * *

Dad was now very well programmed to smoke outdoors. There was a small sea of cigarette butts that attested to his diligence. Once in awhile he would fling a butt into the flower beds. Nothing like a little bit of discarded weed to crank up his elite standing with, "Spade and Dirt Magazine."

"It's your old man dear!" Earl blurted. Melanie's eyes lit up when she saw him. He didn't see those same sparks in anyone else's eyes. Typically, at the office, eyes only perked up when he threw heat. Earl asked the question because he really wanted to know, "How was school?" There were problems in the R.C. High School. In Earl's mind, the problems were blown out of proportion. Of course, in the old cop's mind, if the problem did not involve his immediate family or a dead body; it simply did not meet the cut. It wasn't Earl's fault, just too many damn years of seeing the worst side of folks.

Melanie replied, "Great day Dad … I met a boy!" Earl bit down hard on the scotch—he hated this shit. He knew it could have been worse. After all, there were alternative partners these days. The old staff's mind wandered in the transgression of the moment. "Look at me," how damn sensitive I am! There was a time when the word "partner" almost always inferred a police partner.

Old Dad knew he had to try to communicate with the girl on her ground. The cause was pretty much hopeless with the boy—his mind hovered over boggy ground. Melanie was a different story. She showed a tremendous enthusiasm for life. With some folks, you could just see it in their spirit. Earl cautiously commenced the enquiry, "Does this boy have a future or what?"

"His name is Cody and he is in Grade 11, he plays hockey…."

The old staff made a tangible mental note. Boy and hockey player, just think! He smiled with a sense of fatherly pride. Good girl, not too much detail or dad will race out and run Mr. Love Puck! Judy called out for supper. There was very little conversation at the supper table. The sounds of the distant video game could be heard. Cyber bombs and missiles hurdled throughout the living room. There goes the new flat screen—toasted to bits by a low flying scud.

After the meal, Earl went down to the computer to check out his email. There was no sea of red in the home email. Mostly old fart "MPEG" movies sent from fellow cops. The material could never be classified as porn but every once in awhile.... Melanie and Bob left the house to go out "somewhere." More and more it seemed like "somewhere" was a designated, as opposed to a suggested destination. Earl could hear the distant toss of a "be back time" but they were old enough now. It didn't matter that much. If the kids weren't home as promised, the matter fell by default, to the old man. The double standard was acknowledged in the Jeans' household. Melanie had five minutes of grace and Bob had sixty. It wasn't fair, Earl always acknowledged the obvious—it was reality.

Judy, well Judy ... went up to the bedroom to grade papers. Earl stared at the computer. He really had no intention of checking anything out in particular. He just wanted to corral some of his own space. He thought for a minute about material he could come up with for the boss in Bliss. There was a part of him that was pissed off over the superintendent's scrutiny and yet another, much more twisted side; that loved the corporate sport. Staging the act and perfect execution were critical. He could bring the banker's box file as a prop. He had a couple of thumb drives. He really liked the idea of thumb driving the boss. He would fill the USB drive with mindless spreadsheets, facts and figures from the homicide. It would look, to the naked eye, like he had retained and critically managed tons of vital police information. In the final analysis, he decided to just roll the dice, bring the props and discuss strategy with Kate en route.

There was a humorous "MPEG" that he forwarded to both himself and Kate at the office. He right clicked and checked out the size of the attachment. The gateway police would surely pick off this pup. Funny how the young cops could send spread eagled porn around but just try to sneak in a twisted chuckle! There must be settings on the gateway that were set to "Maximum Density Humor Destruction."

It was now 10:20 P.M., Judy came downstairs. She asked her husband in an unusually sultry and German sounding cabaret voice, "Want some...?"

He replied, "On a school night?" Earl looked at his second cup of whiskey and shrugged. He then looked back at his wife hovering invitingly on the last stair. Clearly, much like waiting rifle recoil, she had positioned herself to retreat back up the stairs with the maximum jolt. There was always the option of throwing back the scotch and thus ruining the subtlety of the moment or, one could simply leave the beverage naked and alone in the dark basement.

If he threw it back, it could mean never crossing the goal line. If he left it alone, the single malt gods would certainly invoke future reckoning. So far, Judy had mentioned nothing about the booze. In a split second test, mixing both pleasure and hope—Earl reached down and downed the scotch. Fuck—he knew he wasn't caught up in a romance novel. He was getting played and liked it very much. Conversation was short lived.

Chapter 6
The Circle

Ernie Moose sat in the cabin. He looked down at the .303 Lee Enfield that he had since 1986. It was Canadian Government issue to the Rangers of the far North. The Rangers were a unit established during World War II to protect Canada's North against a pending foreign invasion. At one point, there were 15,000 Rangers in Canada that were sprinkled throughout current Manitoba, Nunavut and the Yukon. The Rangers were never well organized but formed a legitimate wing of the Canadian military. The goal of the Rangers was to somehow react as a single unit force against an invading army.

Ernie thought the whole idea was funny. "As if" a handful of folks from Wandering Lake could keep an invading army out of Canada. The best they could do would be to call the Rolicking City Police. In order to call the police the phones would have to be working. It was, most days, not very likely. Ernie wondered for a moment if four guys fired .303's at the same time, would it even stop a beat up truck. The old trapper had this rifle for years. He had shot caribou and moose with the weapon. It was always with him on the trap line. Ernie had been involved with the Rangers since he was 22 years old. There was still a smattering of Rangers in Wandering Lake. If the truth ever came to light, there were probably more old Enfield's lost in the bush then there were serving Rangers. The old trapper opened the action and inserted the cleaning rod. He carefully worked the brush and then the cleaning pads. He shrugged

... the rifle should not have been dirty. As he was taught, he put his thumb nail at the breech and looked down the barrel. He wiped down the clip and dry fired the action. Ernie was a long way from home. The old trapper thought about the past couple of days.

Ernie was very well known in Rolicking City. He had spent many nights in the drunk tank. He knew he had a booze problem but it simply could not be helped. He was fine at home but when he came to Rolicking he got trapped in the same old loop. He would have gladly stayed away from the city but there was that damn doctor's appointment. Rolicking City provided the only real hospital for Northern Manitoba. Ernie had a medical appointment for his cough. For most of the civilized world tuberculosis has been wiped out. In Northern Manitoba, the disease remains epidemic.

Ernie went to the hospital three days ago and got a prescription. He was supposed to go back to the hospital yesterday, maybe the day before; hard to remember. He stumbled into the city loop and got drunk. He could not remember how he got there. The only thing that came to mind was that he still had the backpack with the Enfield. The old backpack was, in reality, a large duffel bag. It was the first thing he always checked. His mouth was horribly dry.

He remembered the morning at the dirty, rust colored sink. Hanging from the once chrome taps was the shiny metal link chain which dangled down, stopper-less and without purpose. Affixed to the wall were the remains of broken wall anchors. They were from a mirror that had long since been removed during a middle of the night reno. There was a patch of brighter eggshell white paint clearly outlining the once oval shape of the missing mirror.

The old man looked down at the sink as he spit. He always made sure that the rifle was very well hidden and that it was wrapped tightly in blankets. Ernie was not alone. There were at least eight people in the small hotel room that should only hold two. Most of the sleepers were huddled together on the floor. The scene resembled nothing of a "Roman Orgy," it was the same close huddling characterized in the drunk tank. The situation would look strange to a white man. It could easily be duplicated many times in Wandering Lake. Beds were a luxury. Blankets and possibly a mattress on the floor were deemed a nightly privilege. Huddling did not come about out of a feeling of intimacy. It evolved from a nobler sense of belonging. There existed a greater sense of closeness between his people that the white man would never understand.

The old man looked down at the old black hotel clock. It was so old that the dial actually flipped numbers! Ernie was intrigued and watched the slow roll of the dial to from 11:34 A.M. to 11:35 A.M. The A.M. and P.M. dials were stuck. Much like Vegas, time remained suspended. In reality, there was no reason for a greater sense of day or night. The hours passed as they must. As best Ernie could recollect, he left the room and made his way down the long dark hall. There were old blood stains on the wall and the lobby smelled of piss and beer. A picture of the Rocky Mountains hung geographically displaced in the corner above the old black arm chair. If you were drunk and could make it to the chair—things weren't that bad. In an alley beside the hotel, there were several other people from Wandering Lake.

As was custom, they would insert their hands into their pockets and pull out whatever coins were found. The object of this mission was to purchase some fortified wine. The bottle of wine was less than $8.00 and together they had only a little over $6.00. Ernie's group would have to be patient. The street ritual of collecting for spirits was aptly called, "Chip Ins." The daily ritual was a little like fishing, you had to be patient. There were inherent rules built into the process which were never spoken. The group could not panhandle or they would draw far too much attention. Instead, the circle of friends mingled in the alley sandwiched between the Rolicking Inn and the local soup kitchen. It was a very well known path. The group waited and laughed while an old female elder held onto the cumulative investment.

* * * *

A big male stranger joined the group. The social structure was such that "hand's in pockets" allowed the group to open up the confines of the circle. "Hand's in pockets" was indicative of the presumption that there were coins or, more perfectly—a substantial offering. The male stranger wore the classic black on red checkerboard bush jacket. He spit constantly on the ground in between words. The only thing that had been added to the "classic jacket" over the years was a dangling hoodie. The "red and black" colors were safe for now. They weren't, as of yet, known gang colors. The street people had to watch for the gangsters. They were everywhere yet they were nowhere. The morning and afternoon were safe, conversely the nights, were always saturated with risk. Once the bars closed, it was always much safer to be in cells. There are those that had failed to find refuge in the tank. They had been beaten for coins. Life on the street was tolerated by the will of a greater, much more benevolent force. It was ironic that in the dark, the police were to be sought upon urgent need yet, so skillfully avoided in the sun.

The stranger had a tuft like smattering of hair on his chin. There were no preliminary introductions exchanged, there was instead an ever present sense of greater belonging. There wasn't the complexity associated with conventional social protocol. The stranger pulled out $5.00. The bill was faded white consistent with age and travel—it had made the Northern rounds. The Queen could not begin to imagine the bleakness of her image. The print was faded but still legible on the bill. It was currency for the willing convert. In the greater context, this was the mission of the moment. The old lady holding the total purse made her way to the liquor store on the hill. It was not a voyage that was easily routed. There were always drivers and onlookers who cast their disapproving shadow.

She walked across the road carefully, dressed in jeans and multi layered shirts. A white hoodie popped out awkwardly from beneath the bottom sweater. Her pants were elastic blue and clung closely to her hips. In all likelihood, she would be the only person the liquor store manager would sell to. The locals were very well known to the liquor store staff. A male might pose an implied threat to the cashier but the old lady induced a greater sense of tolerance. Surprising to those outside the circle, there was implicit trust that she would return to the group. The dangers associated with fronting drug money never concerned the circle. They waited out back of the liquor store. Once purchased, the wine had to be consumed very quickly. The biggest risk was during the brief moments of consumption.

There were security cameras out back of the government run liquor store but the group knew precisely where "not" to stand. The pudgy security officer had chased them away many times. The daily ritual of physical repositioning was a strategic exercise founded in trial and error. They were now perched in a safe space where they had seldom been chased from. Street survival always required the unconditional acceptance of the circle's greater sense of knowledge. For the most part, the police were too busy to worry about the street folks. The back alley behind the liquor store was distanced from the road. They could not be easily surprised. If they were caught and spent the night in the tank, they would still be alive. It was not a huge issue. The group was simply not ready for the jail—not quite yet. Custom dictated that refuge from the streets could not arrive until it was aptly due.

There was no issue of who had "chipped in more" than the others. The ritual was goal orientated in concept and in spirit. It was simply a financial action linked to community existence on the streets of Rolicking City. The bottle was passed around in the brown paper bag. The fluid was equally shared and always coupled with laughter and light conversation. The taste was horribly sweet and the consistency much like a dreaded cough syrup. It wasn't really about bouquet, texture or ambiance. It was about achieving a predetermined "city" state of mind.

It was not the conversation of the stock market or RRSP's. It was instead, the incongruent ramblings about the North. Who had been charged by the police? Who were to be best avoided as dangerous? The group laughed out loud. Although, to the outside onlooker; there appeared nothing to smile about. The group always talked about the possibility of danger. This would include the disclosure of safe bush camps, dangerous street folks and especially mean cops. Most of the cops were considered to be just fine.

* * * *

Ernie did not like several of the younger ones. He never understood why they would twist his arm instead of simply asking him to get in the back of the police car. Some cops made him do things he didn't want to. Ernie always got in the back of the car. There was no point taking on the police. In fact, he had spent the night in cells many times. In the end, it was the police that kept him alive. No one that cared had ever found the Enfield. As a Ranger, he had the right to his weapon. The backpack was not very clean. Ernie kept it that way—no one likes to look through filth. It wasn't that good bush dirt either. One time a cop found it in his backpack, it wasn't loaded. He asked me if I was a trapper, and he just wrapped it back up. The morning turned into the afternoon. Ernie could remember very little else….

The trapper did not get up early in the morning as a norm. There was simply no driving need. If he was trapping he would work the line based on the Manitoba Winter. There was either enough sun and warmth or there remained, darkness and cold. Ernie's life was not cluttered with long term plans. His life plan consisted simply of existence on this earth.

This morning Ernie made an exception to his morning ritual. He was up early because he was released from cells. It was still dark. The wake up service at the police station was the best! Later in the morning, he hitched a ride out of the city. He could not get back home to Wandering Lake because it was "fly in." It would be a long time to get home now. He had not gone back to the doctor. Only the hospital could give him the return ticket home. Most of the communities around Rolicking were First Nations communities and were accessible only by air. Most of the year, you took a plane to get around—it was accepted.

The old trapper did not want to go back to the hospital drunk. He knew that the hospital would call the police. There was another reason. The guy with the bush jacket, the stranger with the $5.00 bill, was mad and wanted to fight Ernie. He needed to get the hell out of Rolicking. He was told it was time. The map on his hand would help him find the cabin. The stranger had pushed him, and it hurt. Ernie always knew when to leave the street family. He knew that he was damn lucky to get a ride. A person hitch hiking has virtually no chance of catching a ride in the first place. The old trapper felt fortunate. The fuel delivery truck driver knew him. The North was small and this driver had worked up in Wandering Lake for a year or so. He paid Ernie cash to hand pump fuel into barrels. He would then take the barrels on the snow machine sled and make the rounds. Fuel was often pumped four or five times before it found a final tank.

Ernie remembered looking down at his hand. The make shift map confirmed that he had reached the cabin area of Shallow Lake. Shallow lake was about two hours south of Rolicking City on the way to Bliss Landing. It was a small community with 75 cottages or so spread out on the east side of the lake. The area itself was not politically organized. There were cabins and several dozen permanent houses around the big lake. There was history on Shallow Lake. An old Hudson's Bay fur trading post still stood proudly at Sandy Beach.

The cabin was exactly where it was supposed to be. It was brown with white trim—it was strangely new yet previously seen in vision. There was a prevailing sense of happening at the cabin that was not reflected at arrival. Ernie shook and the ensuing cough took his breath away for several minutes. Getting in through the screened porch door in back was easy. He sat hunched over the kitchen table with both arms resting on opposing chair backs. Ernie could see the lake through a large white framed living room window. The small treed island about 200 yards in the distance looked more like it should be the lake's play toy. Although he knew that he should have gone back to the hospital, he also realized that it made far more sense to get out of the city. Street danger was more imminent than a cough. Something would happen—it always did. He would only get beat up or end up in jail. The tank was one thing—jail time was something totally different.

The old trapper remembered his time in cells after the December fur table. He had sold his fur and exchanged the hides for money. His pockets were lined with the stink of cash. The tank was so crowded he got in a "push fight" with another drunk. Ernie got the worst of it and his face was covered in blood. He could only remember the old cop that entered the cell to get him out. Then the ambulance came and took him for stitches. After the hospital, he got put in a separate cell. It was more like a hotel room than the tank.

Ernie remembered thinking, good thing that I was so drunk or it would have hurt way more. At the same moment he rubbed his chest. He still had a broken rib from that night. It hurt when he coughed. The old trapper thought that it never did heal right—that was almost a year ago. He looked around the cabin. It was cold now, almost -10 degrees during the Manitoba Fall. Autumn never truly happened in Northern Manitoba. It was simply a state of transition and not a defined season. One would typically be comfortable with the late summer sun and then remarkably cold with the onset of change. The leaves on trees often held fast until there was already a foot of snow. It was as of the weather gods had somehow missed an email to the trees.

Ernie could not risk lighting a fire or the neighbor's might see the smoke;

he had been warned. There was also no vehicle out front. Ernie had no problem getting in. He had often broken into cabins when he must. He was not a thief and he obviously had no money. Ernie knew it was not a trapper's cabin in the woods. It was obviously someone's summer home.

Ernie saw the family pictures around the main cabin area. There wasn't much. Most of the people in the pictures were holding up fish. Ernie chuckled, the photos of white folks holding up fish was too much! His rib hurt when he laughed. Ernie looked around the cupboards and found some cookies. Ernie knew winter was coming fast. The sun did not rise until 7:45 A.M. or so. The old trapper had no use for a wrist watch. It would only be taken by those that inflicted pain. He felt very tired and weak, it was the damn ribs. Every time he coughed, it felt like he would pass out.

He wondered if he should try and get back to town and see a doctor while he was sober. There was at least a mile walk to get to the main highway. Ernie did not think he could make it. Although he had broken in through the back screen door, he treated the cabin with respect. Ernie thought out loud, he would take what he needed and sleep a little. It would be safe. He did not mind being alone. The bush never made him feel lonely. There was life all around him. In all likelihood the cabin was already shut down for the winter. Ernie could smell the odor of antifreeze in the toilet. He got up and walked around a little. It was not a big cabin—there were three bedrooms. One of the bedrooms had a small dollhouse and celebrity posters lined the walls. Ernie shrugged and commented while looking at the posters, "Rock Stars, eh!"

He looked under the beds in case there were other guns around. He would not take them but just in case, he needed to clarify their existence. The fridges, one white and one brown, had sticks in the doors. They were obviously shut down for the season. There were some clothes hanging on a round shaped chrome hanger. It looked totally out of place in a cabin. The hanger should rightfully be displayed in a dress store in Rolicking. The only thing that fit right was an old canvas jacket. The jacket was the kind with brown matted fur on the collar. It was olive drab with great big roomy side pockets. It smelled faintly of gun powder. The jacket was very old. Ernie stared at it and memories of his grandfather popped into his head. He removed it from the round hanger. There were no fancy sticky fasteners on the jacket. Only buttons on the outside and a big metal zipper on the inside. The jacket embraced the smell of past owners. He knew that it wasn't the kind of jacket that one man bought. It was a jacket that had hung in the cabin for years and was worn by many. It was in remarkably great shape. It was very heavy and most unlike light modern jackets. Ernie tried it on. He felt immediately warmer and more comfortable. His hands instinctively dug deeper while his fingers probed the inner confines of the pockets.

The trapper found a set of keys and an old Kleenex in the left pocket. He held out the keys. They were old and likely fit padlocks around the property. He cautiously peered out one of the bedroom windows. There was a big, randomly stacked wood pile to the south. Ernie thought that once it was dark he could risk a fire. There would have to be a west wind or the nearby neighbor would certainly smell the smoke. Smoke that lingered in the air divulged much about the location of a stove. Ernie walked out into the porch and smiled. There was an old bicycle and a beat up box busting full of firewood.

Ernie was happy that he had found the right cabin. It looked like a place where there might be more food. There was a child's pail at the front door. The cabin felt safe. It was obviously a very peaceful place.

Chapter 7
The Departure Lounge

Earl walked into the office at 6:30 A.M. The old staff parked the old Ford in the lot and used his security card to enter through the garage entrance. There was a Chevy truck with a "DO NOT TOUCH" sign on the windshield. Earl hated clutter in the garage. The truck was obviously waiting for "Identification Services" (Ident) to fingerprint it. In the big city there would be a proper place for Ident to look for evidence. Up here, they made do with the garage. There were three big garage doors at the back of the office. This time there was only one truck waiting for Ident. There had been times when the bays were all filled up. Earl noticed a boat in one of the stalls. It was Bush's boat, dripping mud off the wheels and onto the floor. Earl thought to himself that Bush would not likely clean up the mess. The slobber would sit and reek until he made it an issue. Earl really did not want to make it a big deal, but he dearly wanted to "zing" the troops.

It was great sport to zing. It wasn't fun to bitch and complain about the obvious but a zing made the point with the noticeable absence of management pretence. Earl rounded second and noted that the ladies washroom was still out of order. That meant that they, the chicks, would be heading downstairs to the locker room can. This was both bad and good news. Bad in the sense that there would be a steady stream (no pun intended) downstairs. Good, because Earl was going on a roadie. Earl walked past the sea, well really a pond of cops working with "B" Watch.

P.B. sat in the ICU Office. There were several RCP already working. Bush was trying to impress the group with your basic reconstituted senior "cop yarn." The pack was joined by the rookie Ron Fleury. As per the norm, the crew was in an animate discussion over the trivialities of modern policing.

Bush always eager to impress shouted across the floor, "Good Morning Staff!" He trumped his salutation with the question, "How those old bones be a rocking?"

Earl smiled and spun back with, "They be rocking just fine once we solve the flower caper." Fleury saw the old staff. He grabbed a file folder and a metal ticket holder. The trick was creating the illusion that you are busy. Earl chuckled to himself, he liked that…. Even at an early age they learn how to smoke management.

Earl could not help but drop a slam. He sniped, "Ron … you in a big hurry to do something important with a red file?" The red files were the RCP bulked ticket files. No reason for them to leave the office. Earl walked over to Fleury and offered, "Here is what you do when you want the boss to think you give a shit." Earl illustrated, "Grab an investigational file, namely a white file, grab your ticket book, put your fucking hat on and then hit the road." Earl auto corrected himself, "Okay, I admit … the hat was a little much. Best case, the hat should already be in your vehicle then I can catch you walking out of the office without it. Then, only then—do I get to give you holy shit."

Ron nervously left the room without saying anything and rounded second. Earl shrugged and thought to himself, guess he wet himself. Earl took great pride in verbal diarrhea. It wasn't how you laid on the shit—it was more the style of the dump. The old staff walked into the coffee room. He found his mug. The day prior he hid it with the damn plastic leftover containers on the lower shelf. Coffee was still there from night shift. Earl didn't care. He dunked his nose in the pot, took a whiff and shook his head. He blurted out, "Killer shit—just the way I like it!"

He walked into his office and launched himself in his chair spinning around like a kid. The chair rotated one complete revolution until it faced his computer. Earl wanted to be able to say that he checked his email before he left. Gretchen could be "Electronic Earl" in a pinch, she had all the passwords. The trouble is … she would be in too late to effectively deploy. Timing was essential as the system logged the open time of the emails. Earl tried to log on, it was always *Rolicking* followed by a number. Earl entered *Rolicking 38*. Case Sensitive bastards Earl thought, yep, that will fool the bad guys. Just hurdle in a cap letter into a password.

Earl often wondered if this was simply a hold back to the days of the

KGB. The system prompted him for a new password every 90 days. As per the ritual he chose *Rolicking 40.* This time, Earl felt that he should bypass 39 and take the big league leap to 40. If he stayed on track and the system made him change his password every 90 days then when he retired he would have *Rolicking 57.* It was, on face value, very trivial shit but Earl cherished "past times" to better motivate himself. Without humor, cop life would certainly spin an otherwise sane man into cross-eyed submission.

The old staff had created games to not only pass the time but in order to cultivate a healthier sense of perception. His thumbs painfully crawled across the keyboard visibly searching for letters. Earl suddenly remembered last night. He picked up his cell and ever so slowly, "one thumb" texted Judy, "Tanx for d action."

At that very moment of texted sentiment with his wife the image of Val with flowers invaded his brain—Judy would certainly not approve. Out damn Rolicking Lips logo, out! Earl refocused on the emails, nothing major. There was one message from M.D. and another from District. Earl read the subject line in disgust, "Pot Luck Fall Supper." Earl right clicked and cyber chucked the email like a pro. As he clicked the mouse he rocked it off the pad. He knew that Judy hated office functions. There was an unwritten rule in the Jeans' household—Earl doesn't do school, and Judy doesn't do RCP functions. Like most standing rules, there were the yearly compromises. A pot luck supper would not meet that cut. Earl started an email addressed to the troops;

Subject: Boat in Garage-Mud Dripping Like Snot
Good Morning!
There is a boat in the garage dripping snot like mud all over my floor. This sucks, it is not right and must be corrected immediately. I don't know who owns this pile of shit. It better be out of here by sundown. After dark, I will set it adrift for good.
Have a nice day. You folks rock but ever so poorly!
Staff Earl

Earl never used rank, he despised it but for the shear ambience and continued zing factor of the narrative an authoritative title was required. He sat back and waited. Bush was in ICU talking to P.B. Without a doubt, he had an alert tone set for a new email. A guy had to know what was coming. Emails in any police force were not only the preferred medium of porn but they also dispensed time sensitive intelligence. Earl thought this is great. Here is a guy always taking center stage but totally oblivious to his own mortality.

Earl picked up his phone and called Kate's cell, "Hey, you around yet?"

Kate answered, "Just heading to the shop."

Earl said, "Just watch from the library and tell me if there is a boat getting hitched up in the garage."

"Would there be any point asking why?"

"Nope, no point, um … call me back once you see the boat getting hitched up."

Kate called five minutes later, "Bush is hitching up the boat."

"What's he hitching it up with…?"

"Echo 82."

Earl hung up and was elated! There was virtually nothing in life that could match the joy of the game. The old staff took a deep breath to settle his excitement. He took his right hand and moved it vertically across his face. His efforts were intended to stop a massive chuckle that was difficult to contain. Someday, Earl pondered, he would definitely require adult diapers. Earl slid through second, stormed through the interior door and crashed into the main garage area.

Earl barked at Bush, "It was you that parked the fucking piece of shit boat in here. What the fuck? What the holy fuck … were you thinking?"

Bush looked silently at Earl as he dropped the safety pin to the hitch. The pin bounced and loudly pinged off the concrete floor, "But I was just going to clean it up…."

Bush didn't complete the words. Earl loaded up another round, "In my fucking garage, right?" Earl thought to himself that the possessive "my" was excellent.

There was no place to go and Bush knew that. Earl couldn't help it—he started laughing out loud. The coffee cup he was holding started spilling all over the cherished floor. Earl said, "Hey, I don't care but the next time you get an email from the boss make damn sure you aren't being set up!" Earl really liked Bush. He was okay, but an open target was fair game. Opportunity missed was a fucked up day for the old staff. Earl knew that in spite of the humorous delivery, the overall context of the message was sent and received. Furthermore, he would get extra mileage because all the troops would rib Bush for days. Earl had this mental image of filthy boat pics sailing into Bush's email!

"Make sure you clean up the fucking mess!" bellowed Earl while exiting stage right into the main office. Kate had sauntered into ICU through the north side wanting to avoid the whole parking lot scene. Kate loved a joke as much as the next cop but not at 7:00 A.M. in the morning. She saw the email on Bush's screen and gave Earl "the look." It was something that Kate had truly mastered over the years. She was both a cop and a chick ... she could telepathically chuck shit at will.

Earl fired, "Hey if I wanted to see that look I would just go home."

Kate retorted, "Judy's got squat on my bitch gaze!"

Earl said, "Grab your shit so we can hit the road."

Chapter 8
The Flag Girl

Kate and Earl spun through the local drive thru. At the moment of entry into the string of vehicles, Earl remembered the boys getting stuck. He never did get around updating the rule book.

Earl commented, "Shit, the boys got stuck here the other day."

Kate, "Yeah I heard, it was bound to happen at some point."

Earl, "It just looks so damn bad. I can see why they would think the bad guy was long gone. It's just that … they treated the whole thing like sweet fuck all."

Kate uttered into the galvanized box, "One large black and one cream and sugar." Kate turned and asked, "Ya want something to eat?"

Earl piped up like a little girl, "Let's get some moon bites for the road and something for the Sir. I'm thinking some gingerbread men or something like that—that'll crank him."

Kate ordered, "A small box of moons and a half dozen gingerbread men."

Earl chirped up, "Sure would like to see you eat a gingerbread man."

Kate never missing a beat, "Yeah, bet you would. I would eat it damn slow starting at the fucking head then I'd throw the rest to the dogs."

Earl, "Geez, Bitch I think I'm in love." Earl and Kate had sparred for years. It kept them alive. You won't find this type of therapy in any self help book. Cops thrive on the syntax jabs and metaphor kicks, all good. Earl often thought that it was all the banter that kept semi-sane cops so mentally sharp. He never read a study on it or anything but he knew, deep down, it kept him fine tuned. Like a ... well nothing came to Earl—that was very odd.

The duo took their order and double checked the coffee lids. Seasoned cops always check the coffee lids. Earl had a suit on because he knew that Kate would be in civilian attire. How dumb would it look for him to be in a Rolicking monkey suit and Kate in her fine looking "haute couture." The old staff looked at Kate. It bugged him a little that she was driving. They grabbed the ICU unmarked Crown Vic and of course, Kate already had the keys.

This was not Earl's plan. He was looking forward to a cigarette and coffee en route. He should have insisted on the old Impala but after the boat thing with Bush, he was still relishing his post coital high. Earl truly enjoyed this buzz it was much better than bad sex but not as good as shooting a moose in the nose. It was a rule, actually chiseled in the rule book. Smoking was not permitted in police vehicles. This decree was at least ten years old now and originated from the lofty heights of Mindless Bliss.

Earl blurted, "Fuck ... guess, I can't smoke in this beastie!"

* * * *

Kate sipped her coffee while negotiating the drive thru exit. She was short and to the point, "Good." She elaborated, "I'll stop in an hour and you can suck on a smoke." The detective took a little time to negotiate the final turn out of the drive thru. For some reason, there was a pedestrian cross walk that went across the drive thru. It was at a curve, in the worst part of the exit forming a natural blind corner. Kate brought the vehicle to a complete stop; just in case. It was cold out now in the mornings. There was often an icy trail generated by the early morning coffee crowd.

Kate looked down at the box of gingerbread men. She wondered to herself if Earl had thought about this all night, or what. The detective really liked Earl. For a guy he was "obsolescent gray" attractive. He really didn't evoke total oblivion like some old guys. He fell somewhere in between the rest home crowd and that guy in the "infomercials." Kate had dabbled with the proverbial "other team" for awhile. It wasn't a big deal in her mind but she had played house with Coral. Her roommate was a local teacher that worked with Judy. There was the expected town chatter but in the North most lifestyles eventually become accepted. Kate was smart enough to know that in her current role, who she jumped was everyone's business. Living with another woman was not all that it was cracked up to be (no pun). Kate knew going into the shack up with Coral that it was driven by a greater sense of loneliness rather than that "cop presumed" social de-evolution.

Coral and Kate were not coed's in some Vancouver college. Hell they weren't even French. In fact, if the truth be known … the whole episode was much rougher on Coral. Working at the High School, she was often the target of some inconsiderately fired off color remarks. Kate never cared about the talk. She cared more about the "non-talk." This was especially true amongst cops. When cops chucked shit things were fine. When cops were silent in the room fucking, beware.

Kate finally sprung herself from the donut lane. She hit a ruby (red light) and got a little hung at the intersection. Her mind had wandered and she knew it. The Ford was at a dead stop six feet into the intersection.

* * * *

Earl said nothing and chomped at a "moonie." Like a guy trying not to get caught ogling porn in a plane, his eyes shifted to anything non Kate. Earl could see the flower shop in the distance. He wondered to himself what Val would be wearing. He liked the fact that he had company for the ride. He wanted to talk with her about the break up with Coral, but he didn't really know how to bring it up. It would have to wait. It was a topic that needed some build up miles of foreplay before a guy could reasonably work "naked relations" into the conversation. After all, the old staff was not so unsophisticated, as he lacked good taste.

Earl took a great deal of pride in the fact that he was socially challenged. He really didn't care at all. Conversely, Judy always gave a damn and that kept her always on edge. Earl could utter anything at any time—it was the privilege of age. He had tenure with the RCP. The worse the city could do is force him to retire early. In the meantime, he would very happily chuck shit!

Earl stared down and a little bit of powdered sugar hit his tie. He blurted out, "For fucks sakes!" He took a tissue from the box and spit on it. He then proceeded to try and rub the sugar out. It only made it worse. Little bits of the tissue disintegrated into the tie. There was a swirl in the middle comprising a multitude of offending colors. Behind the swirling colors and blended, every so skillfully; was a very non-pronounced, "Fuck You." It was totally subliminal. The receiving target almost had to know it was there. Kate had known for several years about the tie but no one else knew but Judy. Earl would consider no other tie for District other than the "FYT."

* * * *

Kate looked across the shotgun rack and back down to Earl's tie. She commented, "Now don't you be rubbing out the "U" or some other important letter because that would suck!" Kate snapped her head back and redirected her attention. She immediately felt a little awkward glaring at anything "Earl" that was not above the shoulders.

The duo had just blazed the last traffic light in town. The sun was coming up slowly now. They were now driving due south. Kate caught the sunlight in her left eye and immediately swung the visor to her side window. Once you booted out of the city, it was now an officially sanctioned road trip! The detective thought quickly about the statement she had to take. It was a follow up statement for the robbery at the Co-op. An individual had walked in the convenience store with a knife demanding cash. He took some other small items. Bush had taken the statement, it was a mess. Kate didn't even tell Earl about the problems with the statement. The Crown Attorney had called as Kate knew she would. The detective really didn't understand how anyone could interview a victim of any crime and miss all the basics. Bush wasn't alone. He was there with another cop. Sometimes "two's" of things doesn't make it better. Kate hated to go over old ground and waste time. Missing from the statement was virtually no description of the suspect.

She thought of the question asked by Bush, "What did the individual look like?"

The store owner Jason McIvor replied, "Like he came from the bush."

The next question asked was, "What time did all this happen?"

Kate thought, you would think that even normal folks would try and revisit the description before moving on to a time frame. There was something very mind numbing about the new cops. Kate could not put her finger on it, but maybe they weren't in the job. She had tried to rationalize the missing pieces but there simply weren't any answers. Maybe they need more training. Maybe they suffered from a warped series of bad days. She found herself talking out loud, "Maybe a bad life, that's it."

Earl turned to the driver, "Hey, you talking to yourself again?"

Kate, "Not like I have anyone to talk with…."

Earl asked, "How things goin' on the home front?"

Kate knew that she had strolled into her partner's catching mitt. She clarified, "It's going. It'll just take some re-jigging on my part. It was no one's fault. Just didn't pan out, that's all."

Earl offered, "You know, Judy always thought the world of Coral."

Kate hit the brakes hard: the Crown Vic swerved back and forth from the rear. Rocks flew and banged off the sides of the car. Earl instinctively cupped his left hand over his lid while hunching forward out of crotch splashing range. Kate glanced in the rearview mirror while coffee eked out from the air holes in the coffee lid.

Kate really didn't know why she was so worked up. It was just too soon and she sure as shit wasn't in the mood to hear "kudos" for the ex. The Crown

Vic dipped forward and ground to a stop. Kate turned to Earl and welded her eyes to Earl's face.

* * * *

Earl hadn't felt a visual probe like this since his last medical. The old staff had no idea how he fucked up; he just sensed—he must have. A sick feeling churned in his gut. Whenever he played the "good guy" an innocent person almost always got hurt! The accumulated interest earned with having a non editing personality often caught up to him. The old staff knew that he had to regroup and a throw a rope to the old Earl. That's it, haul the shot chucking, mouth spitting, red faced, in your face Earl quickly back to the boat! Earl was ablaze in the myriad of options. It was absolutely critical what came next. At the same time, he wondered why she would not let up that damn glare. While eyeballing Kate's gun, Earl's lips quivered and built up gradual tempo.

Consistent with his resolve to do right; he said, "I could kiss you now!" Kate shot more stare and Earl hoped like hell that his attempted diffusing mechanism had worked. He looked down and was suddenly very conscious about the gun on her hip. In reality, he didn't catch the whole gun, just the grip and a bit of holster. Any other normal guy would simply see the handle of a gun. To a guy cop partial "piece" was little bit like seeing bra strap.

* * * *

Kate held the steering wheel "white knuckled tight." She leaned farther to the right and remained motionless. Kate's gaze gradually lessened intensity. She observed for the first time that Earl had a long hair growing out of his left ear. She started to laugh out loud. It was not a wee follicle. It was a hair that should have been plucked long ago by said keeper.

Earl chirped up, "Geez that was a close call did a rat cross the road or what…?"

Kate looked down. Luckily, there was not much damage to her Rolicking fashion suit. It was a blouse, blazer and pants ensemble that she had found in a junky local outlet. It fit well and Kate liked that. Most of her clothes were too damn snug. They were in between throwing them the fuck out or tolerating the discomfort. The trouble was, too many of her clothes now fell into the latter category.

Kate had worn a size "11/12" for years. She would never buy a bigger size in Rolicking. If she had any down time in Bliss she wanted to hit a few stores. Kate thought to herself, while Earl is catching shit … I can buy a few things. She knew she would have to rip all the tags off or Earl would certainly check the size. The other option was to never let any of her clothing purchases out of sight. She couldn't even put them in the trunk. Like most police vehicles the trunk was filled with dirt, hype needles, a questionable spare tire, a flashlight with dead batteries, an empty windshield washer jug, a shovel with a useless little handle, a length of rusty chain, one jumper cable, dirty exhibit bags, a fire extinguisher that needed charging, a first aid kit with one gauze pad and last, but not least, an old body bag. It's not like a body was in the bag but you never knew the whole history. There could very well be pieces of a person. Everyone knew that—so the bag just lived in the trunk. When you really needed a clean body bag you would get one at the hospital or the funeral home.

Kate refocused her attention on driving. Oddly, it was a very nice sunny morning. There had been lousy weather for the last few months. The sun was intensely warm. It rose up in the sky very quickly and eventually out of her eyes. Kate put her hand down and switched over police radio channels. She keyed the repeater and got the Telecom Center in Bliss, "This is 4 Tango Papa en route to Bliss—Staff Jeans and Detective Kate O'Malley from Rolicking."

The male dispatcher replied, "Good morning and thank you."

Earl and Kate looked wildly at each other. They were not used to such a polite and friendly Telecom's Operator. They both felt a wave of utter disbelief. Strangely, Earl felt disappointed. He actually looked forward to commenting on the presumed rude behavior. Without knowing it, the dispatcher had taken the wind from Earl. This was not easily accomplished. Earl out of impulse snapped, "What a phony fucking polite asshole thing to say."

Kate nodded in approval, "Yeah a new guy...."

The side window was open a small crack. Earl did it out of habit hoping that Kate would let him smoke. In the old days this was "do able." Earl could easily exhale cigarette smoke while spitting sunflower seeds out a one inch crack. The team passed the Rolicking dump and they were briefly held up by construction. The roads in the North were never very good. Earl accepted them for what they were. Cracked windshields were perfectly normal. There were only three dings in the Crown Vic. The dings would connect the dots over winter. Typically, the windshield would be replaced in the spring. No one would ever dream of replacing any windshield with four dings. This was now the coveted time to pick up some gratis whacks. It was indeed, bonus time! Earl asked, "Where do you think the next one will hit?" He pointed to a previously hit area of glass.

Kate obviously over her hostility, replied in a very scientific voice, "Well Staff, the projectile will hit at a 30 degree angle just above the steering wheel. Then it will carom right past your left eye. It will hit a pole then nail your right ear through the open window."

Kate could not get the image of that damn ear hair the hell out of her mind. She thought to herself, would he just let it grow and grow? Surely Judy would notice, married folks … maybe not. She would have to wait awhile and then plant the information with one of Earl's kids. That's it, sitting on something like this was not easy but some things in life are just worth the wait. She could never waste a mutant follicle comment without the appropriate target audience. Kate could not believe that she had exercised so much damn control at the time of discovery. If she slipped and mentioned it, the hair would be plucked immediately—she would lose her edge forever.

The Crown Vic with Rolicking's finest had just passed a road sign, "Hill Mountain 75 km." They were going at a good clip: the road was dry but rough. They pulled up to a flag girl who was the daughter of Sergeant Mike Funk. Mike was the Operational NCO and he fell directly under Earl.

As they pulled up Kate lowered the passenger window, "Hi Ashley, how you doing?"

Ashley responded, "Great, we are finally out of the bugs and into the cold."

* * * *

This would likely be the final week of road work. Earl stared at the teenager. Ashley was 16 years old. She had not as yet returned to school. The Operational Sergeant was often referred to simply as the "Ops NCO." There were no Captains, Lieutenant's or Commanders at the Department. You were either a constable or a NCO. Earl thought he had it bad in the office some days. In practice, a lot of the day to day havoc, legal issues and people problems were pushed down to Mike. Earl liked to keep busy but in the office sense—he deemed himself the "master pusher."

Funk was a hard guy with a semi-permeable inner core. Mike had been hard on Ashley growing up. His daughter was not destined for greatness or a university education but Earl did like the fact that she was working. Earl sized up the kid looking up and down. Shit, his Melanie would never be caught dead in "non designer" overalls. Hard hat and ear muffs working the great outdoors was not an enviable summer job. There was nothing "designer" about this girl. She came complete with the "issued piercings." Nothing major but something dangled from her lower lip as if to say, "This will leave a big fucking ugly hole some day." Earl wondered how she could eat a steak with that kind of hardware in place. Some things the old staff had just grown to accept. A year ago, he got in an outright war with his son over a piercing. Behold, in an ear at that! Earl knew he had totally "spazzed" out over the issue. Face it, an earring these days is truly sweet fuck all. Instead of flipping out, Earl knew that he should have simply put his arm around the boy and took him to the piercing joint. Like a hockey banquet or your first peeler, it was one of those missed father and son rites of passage. Things have certainly changed over the last year. Earl truly hoped that the only piercings that Melanie ever inflicted were the ones he could see! This was, after all, any dad's secret wish for his daughter. For a dad and a cop it was once again—an absolute. Earl always thought that if the boy screwed up, he would always have Melanie. He would have to make damn sure he hung in there with her.

Kate and Ashley continued the conversation. "How is your dad doing?"

Ashley replied, "He is doing just fine."

Kate probed, "Enjoying his time off?"

Ashley clarified, "He is actually climbing the walls."

Earl listened intensively. He loved the fact that Mike was climbing the walls. That will teach him to fess up to a shrink! Earl broke up the girls' conversation in mid-stream, "Howz the delay going?"

Ashley picked up her portable radio, "When can I let south bound go…?"

A voice responded, "It'll be about five minutes—just backing in the dump truck."

Earl could not help himself from gawking at the lip ring. It was like the Rolicking lip's tank top but without the "uplifting" visual nudge. It was a weird ring completed at the vortex of protrusion by a little round blue plastic ball. Earl pondered do they keep these things in all night? Could you brush your teeth or would the bristles get stuck in the metal?

The Rolicking Police had been lucky. None of the cops in the office had pushed the issue. Earl was dead set against metal in cops' mouths. The thought was firmly entrenched in the staff's mind. Tangible explanation number one, the metal would clank on the microphone. Better still, it could catch sunlight or a flashlight beam at a crime scene. Now there's a solid officer safety angle!

Earl and Mike jointly managed the office based on the premise that lip rings, did in fact, pose an "officer safety hazard." Earl knew that it was a distant reach but nevertheless, there were more officers in favor then disfavor. The key management strategy was establishing guidelines that were both effective and positively received by most of the rank and file. Earl had the "Bliss Landing Police Association" (BLPA) to also consider. The truth of the matter, there were bigger issues right now. Grooming was not a big deal. At that moment, Ashley signaled Kate and Earl down the road.

Earl commented, "Good kid. I feel so much better after hearing that Mike is climbing the walls."

Kate rebounded, "Ya, I knew that would make your day."

Mike Funk had been, more or less, sent to a psychologist. The sergeant started the medical ball rolling and the shrink finished the job. In the end, further medical evaluation had been ordered by the "Sir" in District. It had been the eventual culmination of many tirades in the office. There was simply no choice. Mike had been on "sick leave" for about two weeks now. Earl resented the fact that he was now doing two jobs. Consistent with the philosophy of never giving a shit, the RCP never back filled a vacant position. So in the interim, everything management—now fell to Earl. Oddly, the RCP paid "acting pay" if you worked a rank above. However, when you did your job and the sick cop who was a rank below, you got squat. Earl never could see the logic, two jobs are two jobs. The domino out of position was becoming the norm. Cops were dropping like flies all over the North. They were drinking too much, flipping out too much and in general, taking things to the "extreme." Police work was an extreme sport without the benefit of a bungee cord. Earl wasn't exactly sure what "extreme" represented but he knew that there were members on the RCP, who were playing out their very private version.

Earl had his own personal version of extreme in his younger days. Earl was always glad that Judy had come in the picture or things would have certainly evolved very differently. The old staff could remember the day that Funk flipped out. By anyone's standard, it was your basic Wednesday morning. Earl reflected that Mike had come into the office already agitated.

Earl had simply commented, "Whatz up your ass?"

Mike replied, "My business."

Earl remembered thinking, that's weird shit. "My business" as opposed to, "Fuck off and die" presented a problem. Furthermore, no cop takes a jab without upping the cheap shot anti. "My business" inferred an intentional retreat into personal space. Cops simply don't do that unless there is a problem.

Earl was not a shrink, so at the time he did not make a big deal of it. About ten minutes after this conversation, P.B. walked into Mike's office. P.B advised the sergeant that his "better half" was pregnant and accordingly, he would be taking paternity leave. Paternity leave was a very interesting evolution with the RCP. The provincial government had deemed it appropriate and the Provincial Police had adopted it too. As with most things in the policing world, the Department was the last to get onboard. Earl looked back fondly at maternity leave. About 15 % of the total RCP was female. Twenty years ago it was probably 5% at best. When a female took mat leave it was obviously to have a baby. Everything considered this makes perfect sense. You are having and then caring for a baby. Probably, you should be at home. Pointing guns, jumping over fences and drinking with the boys would obviously be out of the question! Paternity leave, Earl surmised, was born out of a very well intentioned premise that guys should be at home too. Probably, the first pat leave experience was a guy going home to be with the kid so that the wife could go back to work. Social fucking harmony, Earl thought to himself. The old one sensed that he had shared his solo introspective analysis far too long. Earl asked spontaneously over the chorus of banging gravel, "Kate, what do you think about paternity leave?"

Kate had learned to expect Earl to shift gears pretty much at will. This time was a far reach. Kate tried to clarify, "I thought we were talking about Funk?"

Earl fired back, "Yeah we are, I mean were ... but it's all connected."

Kate nodded and took a sip of cold coffee. "Can you pass me a moonie?" while indicating with a head flick towards the back seat. Earl leaned over and reached behind Kate. He lifted out the box of edibles. Kate reached into the box while she blindly probed to find the right one, "sans powder." Earl watched painfully for awhile. He knew she really wanted chocolate and tossed one to her.

Kate reminisced, "Yep I sure do remember that morning. The same day the rookie started, first shift. I never saw a stapler bang off someone's head like that...."

According to Departmental legend, the moment P.B. highlighted the paternity leave issue, the stapler sailed through the air. It landed just over P.B.'s right eye, striking the orbital bone. If you were into bloodletting this would be the preferred bone of choice. Everyone including the clerks at the front desk heard the thud of the impact. Earl figured even the folks in the cell block must have heard the whack. P.B. dropped to his knees while the six cops on the floor stared on in disbelief. The impact totally destabilized the office. Computer "mice" dropped in mid air and smashed to the floor. In utter disbelief, double latté caramel whipped cups of coffee tumbled from their clutching grips! There was nothing in the rule book that could even begin to cope with "assault with an office instrument." P.B. was dazed by the hit and walked out of the Op's Office clutching his eye. Earl came around the corner and into the main office.

P.B. cried out coupled with bitch tears, "The fucker threw the god damned stapler at me!" It was, by any standard, a very solid wound. Blood streamed out from between P.B.'s fingers. Earl had mixed emotions. He remembered thinking, fucking tears? Tears on a cop in the office were wrong on so many levels. Damn wrong—no one was dead—simply no place for tears.

Earl took charge of everything, no choice. He would always remember the look on Gretchen's face. It was the look of a seasoned clerk who had just been poured over the top. She stood up and just stared at Funk with the rest of the pack. Earl could remember yelling towards the mob on the floor, "Take him to the hospital." He then turned to Funk, "Now you go the fuck home till we figure out how to keep your damn job." It was spur of the moment stuff. Earl probably would have said something different now but then, he just fired from the heart.

In hindsight, the comment implied to the troops that he would do something to keep Funk working. Earl knew he didn't really care. In fact, to get a new cop in the sergeant's seat would actually be of huge value to the office. He didn't want to peg out his remaining years with some dysfunctional SOB. The old staff knew that he had more than enough "dysfunction" in his own life to more than meet the collective needs of the Department.

Earl commented, "Yeah, I didn't see the stapler hit, but I'll never forget the bloody mess."

Kate replied, "Well, I sort of saw it but it was through the open door."

No one in RCP ever closed an office door, it simply never happened. Folks would discuss all types of problems from marital, work, sex, training, promotion, kids, school, harassment and you name it. Those that had the luxury of working in office space with a functioning door would always keep it open. Earl wasn't really sure why this was the case. The open door concept probably stemmed from years of working on the floor in a very open and bullshit laden environment. To this day, Earl wasn't crazy about having his own office. He was not into private space at all. If he wanted tranquility he would go to the cabin by himself. Conversely, he also knew that his role often required some sort of physical barrier from the troops. The only reason for self captivity was to buy more time to move paper. He also liked the idea of the constables not looking over his shoulder to see emails. For the most part, the emails were just so damn belittling and stupid. Earl actually received very little porn, but he liked to create the illusion that his "in box" was plenty "O" skin.

The day of the flying stapler, the door had been open too. Kate elaborated, "Yep I saw the flash of bright and dull metal sail through the air then, P.B. went down." Cops were used to lots of yelling in the office. Typically most discussions, even heated ones, would fall short of projectiles.

Earl said, "Like why the fuck didn't he just slug him or something?" He continued, "I mean, if you are that pissed off, just come around your desk and get into it. A stapler well, that's just bitch fighting at best. He deserves everything the machine can throw at him."

Kate said, "Well ... for the time being he is still getting paid."

No easy answers here. P.B. did the right thing and did not pursue criminal charges. Mike also did the "supposed" right thing and went to the shrink. Earl and Kate did not know all the details, no one did. Earl figured it was a classic case of "establishing" a concrete link to work related stress. Blame the system for your outburst and get into the penalty box for awhile. The whole matter was now in a state of limbo pending medical reports and an internal review board. Funk could still get canned and yes, there were several "choice" jobs that Earl could give him. For sure, he could not wear the Ops hat again. What would be next, sailing paper clips or key boards? Staples are relatively light but there is some distinct weight to a police stapler. The "Arenco Model 15" stapler could punch through 20 sheets of paper. It presented itself as a formidable foe.

Earl brought up another issue, "I can't wait till I read the Workplace Health and Safety report. It will probably be something like,

---

The Arenco Model 15 stapler has been deemed to be an office instrument hazardous for continued use. Although, it represents a capable paper fastening device when hurled from the human hand, it can cause severe injury.

---

* * * *

Kate laughed as her coffee waived precariously above the steering wheel. This was Earl's best trait, she thought. He saw the system for the one-eyed ogre it truly was. She was also certain that the focus of management resolve would also be with the stapler. Kate trumped Earl with a, "Yeah not only will they fire out a report but they will spend thousands of dollars in Bliss looking for another fastening device that cannot be hurdled. I guess this means that we will all have to use those idiot automatic staplers on the photocopy machine. They never work worth shit. You would have thought that an automatic stapler on a police photocopier would have a speed loader or a staple clip. Something, you know, that cops could better relate to!"

"Back to pins," Earl piped up.

Kate, "Pins?"

Earl, "Yep, when I started believe it or not there was a limey sergeant that used to pin paper together."

Kate not missing a beat, "Guess, they stopped that 'cause someone must have lost an eye!"

* * * *

The crew continued down the road superficially absorbed in the autumn scenery. Earl thought this was the real reason why he stayed in the North. Rolicking could live up to its iconic name and the office could be a total mess. Funny thing, once you left town—you were truly disengaged. The escape was very fast yet at the same time, the sentiment prolonged. Time stood still outside of the city. Oddly, Earl did not consider himself a "sensory" kind of guy. The trouble was, sensory or not, the bush was truly overwhelming.

Earl detested going to Bliss. There were always necessary things to buy in civilization but purchases didn't justify the management induced misery.

Kate turned to Earl, "You in deep thought or something?"

Earl replied, "I don't do deep thought."

Kate probed a little more, "So how is Melanie's love life ... she is at that age now?"

Earl knew that Kate was trying to crank him. He really didn't mind, after all; he started the love ball rolling with the Coral chaser. Kate's cranks in a solo situation were actually kind of nice. He knew that his partner was a kind hearted person. She had, more or less, become part of the family herself. Most Christmas' she spent with them. When she was still with Coral, they both came over. The kids thought nothing at all about "who" is jumping who. Earl often thought that kids don't complicate their lives with social judgment. They either like you or they don't—nothing complicated about that.

Kate and Judy got along just great. Not, in the skin book sense with keisters sparking in the night but more consistent with confidants. It was always a tough balancing act. Should Judy really know everything about the office? When Earl came home, he had absolutely no desire to discuss work. Judy on the other hand, wanted to know it all. Almost everyone in town hears something about the players behind the crimes. If it happened in Rolicking, Judy longed for the inside scoop. Earl would not sleep until there was total disclosure. He pondered ... when Kate and Judy talked about the office, it was in a way that was intensely female. However when Earl spoke with Kate it was acronym laden, gun wielding and cuss popping diction! Work talk between cops is response driven while cop talk at home is all about the party line.

Earl would never understand females totally. It was understandable—simply nature's intent. It was as if they derived more enjoyment from the act of conversation than the value of information exchanged.

Earl snapped out of his analytical moment, "Yeah Melanie is seeing some guy. All that I know is that he plays hockey."

"That's it?" Kate questioned.

"Well, that's about all I got offered up," Earl shrugged off the line of questioning.

Kate said, "I guess once you got that far with Melanie you were happy not to confirm anything further."

Earl looked out the side window and thought for a second, "Bang on! It's not that I did not want to find out some more stuff—I do have questions. It's just that I was happy that she offered up the hockey player thing. I didn't want to slip up and have things blow up. Perhaps you are aware; this was a real possibility...!"

Kate replied, "Well done, my learned friend!"

The police vehicle finally tossed the gravel and hit pavement. The car went from banging rocks to sub sonic air flight over the ups and downs of a heaving Manitoba roadway. Kate put the pedal down and pushed the car over 130 kilometers. It was nice to enjoy the last few weeks of ice free roads. It would not be long before things went for a dump. Trips out of Rolicking almost always meant an aircraft in the winter. You could drive to Bliss but it was a crap shoot at best. A small red fox with a mouse clamped in its mouth scurried across the road.

Earl commented, "Well, he got the hell out of your way."

Kate replied, "Guess he heard about that rat—you think you saw!"

Chapter 9
Under the Bridge

Like gravel shoulders and bugs, wildlife are a huge part of Manitoba. Travelers take their fellow Northerners for granted. Moose, black bear, fox and the odd lynx most frequently grace the trail. That was one of the reasons the staff kept the rifle in the pickup. You just never know what could be out there. Earl wasn't one to poach game, but he wouldn't be inclined to pass it up either. Like any outdoorsman, you continually scope out opportunity and take note of future possibilities. Since the beginning of the summer, Earl had kept track of a big bull moose that was about five kilometers from the cabin. He saw it by the road in April and tracked it in June. He knew that the big bull would not roam far. In the old days, Earl hunted with a group of buddies. Now he would probably buy a tag and do the solo thing. He was at home in the bush. There was very little that he could not adapt to and coexist with.

Kate commented, "Well, another 52 kilometers to Hill Mountain."

Earl replied, "Slow down, we'll only get there too soon. You wanna go shopping or something?"

The staff was firmly in "cabin withdrawal." He went to the cabin constantly over the summer. Now, it was pretty much closed down for winter. Earl would naturally still head out but with no running water the rest of the family would likely pass up the call. Earl worried about the fate of the cabin. Bob was not after all, the kind of kid to keep up future maintenance. Melanie enjoyed working with her dad but he knew that boys and social convention would eventually win out. Judy had absolutely no idea about any of the deemed, "guy jobs" at the cabin. The only question she ever posed was, "Is the toilet working?" If there was water, Judy would go. If there was no water she would pass—nothing complex in her world.

Earl really didn't mind. In fact, since the kids were older he could just head off by himself. He cherished the fact that the phone did not ring in the woods. There was a phone service available but he had refused for years to put one in. It just made no sense in Earl's mind to have a phone in the bush. The whole idea was … he wanted *not* to have human contact. Conversely, if there was an emergency, he knew that he would certainly be on his own.

As a cop, he knew everyone at the Hospital, Fire Department and of course, the Police. If he had a heart attack at the cabin, he would have to simply sit down and die. Of course, fully versed in first aid, he knew enough to take aspirin and then croak. Even if he had a phone, calling for help looking goofy or being naked could never happen. He secretly hoped that he would never meet the Grim Reaper curled up in some twisted action position. He had seen folks die on toilets and in bathtubs. Worse case, he would have to stop, flush and roll off the toilet.

The old staff knew, that the fact that he even thought about the finalities of life was, extremely off centered. It was virtually impossible for a cop not to think of the inevitable. Normal people have the luxury of pondering the "ways and means" of their future demise. A cop longs simply, for the simplicity of a polished exit. There were just too many calls where good folks met up with bad timing. You could easily die from a bullet or by the deadly swipe of a two-ply wipe.

Earl used the cabin to defuse. Sure as shit, if there was a phone the office would be calling. I mean, fellow cops never care. It wasn't even about required communication. It was all about the shifting of responsibility to a superior. Most of the time when Earl received a call, it truly mattered not. He could not remember the last time he got a query that was fully worthy of submission. He then thought, it was the call about the murder.

Earl thought about the body. "Kate, how is the murder coming?"

Kate replied, "You read the report."

Earl asked, "Ya, but can we solve this one?"

It was becoming a sore point with Bliss and the community of Rolicking. There was a gang element in the North now. This murder was no different than the last three. The North was now violent and spontaneous. A body had been found under the bridge going north out of the City. It was ripe with gas. It had been partially emerged in the water for awhile. There was a single gunshot to the back of the head. The hollow point bullet mushroomed in the skull. Consistent with close range, the powder residue on the back of the head was tight and concentrated. The hollow point round was intended to kill immediately and possibly, disfigure on exit. It's often difficult to tell what a hollow point will do. It could just mushroom and destroy tissue or it could retain enough momentum and end up nearby. One shot was obviously more than enough to get the job done. Consistent with conscious recycling, no brass was found in the area. Earl got the call early around 5:00 A.M. A local dumpster diver had stumbled across the scene. Under the bridge was always a casual meeting place for those that evaded the formality of the boardroom.

When the staff got to the scene, Kate was already there. She had a couple of uniforms and P.B. was with her. These types of investigations never come with a hot trail. The victim originated from Winnipeg and was a very well known gang member. He was known on the street simply as "8 Ball." Earl didn't know the whole story behind the handle. In all likelihood, 8 Ball came to a gun fight horribly under armed. Possibly, just a pool ball stuffed in the toe of a sock. Investigations like these would traditionally be solved by "the proverbial call."

In the old days, a body would arrive with a story. Earl could remember his first homicide. It was in the local bar. One brother killed another over a six pack of beer. That was the story and the whole bar had witnessed the stabbing. Nowadays, no one killed around witnesses. Earl knew that the brass expected this one solved. Rolicking had grown weary of the headlines, *Cops still out there looking for clues.* The media lines had actually grown closer to reality. Kate and her crew were doing their best. Earl could not help but think, "Who gives a fuck?" He must have said it out loud.

Kate uttered, "I do." Earl was doing some classic mental gear shifting. Melanie was now out of fourth gear and the murder was in overdrive.

Earl probed, "So what's your thinking on the murder?"

Kate, "Classic dope thing, I guess." She elaborated, "You know, we see these things time and time again. You have a body with a sordid past, and you have a hole in the puke's head. It's not the stuff of murder mysteries anymore." Kate was on a roll…. "We get the body and zero history of the person behind the body. We know that 8 Ball was all over the North and in deep with *Alliance*. He had Alliance tats all over his body. The classic "ALL" was tattooed across the webbing of his left hand. The brass in Bliss will never understand the reality of Rolicking crime we have to."

Earl completed the sentiment, "Yeah, you're right those Alliance mother fuckers are running the show now."

There was a time when all the violence would have been harnessed in Winnipeg or Bliss Landing. Now, Rolicking was far too "beat up." There was money to be made in the drug trade that warranted the trip up the road.

Economic opportunity always provided a ripe venue for criminal investment. Why would you peddle any type of dope in Bliss when you could drive up the road and sell it for a 30% mark up? Earl understood the economic variables behind the problem. For the citizens of Rolicking, their city was now perceived as simply too damn easy. They looked back fondly at a community that could no longer be.

In reality, the focus of the violence was contained between the gangs. There was the presumption of cause and effect. A body could literally surface anywhere. Very few working people were ever victims of crime in Rolicking. The ugliness was most often contained within the gangs and to a certain extent, the street folks. Earl thought about what he could possibly tell the superintendent that would make a difference? The Mayor knew the problem but she answered to the voters. All the voters knew was the violence perpetrated in the coffee shop and media. Perceived crime was actually worse than real crime. Cops can target real crime but seldom the greater intangibilities of inspired crime.

Chapter 10
The Cabin

Ernie fumbled with the keys. It was now dark. He walked out slowly exiting from the south side door of the porch. He felt fortunate that there was not three feet of snow on the ground. As he walked down the steps, a big owl flew into the trees. Ernie did not like the owl—it was an omen. The owl was white and grey. It had weight in flight that left a most solid impression. The displaced cold air could be heard swooshing under the large wings. Ernie thought, there must be some good hunting around the cabin. The old trapper walked across the cabin lot while glancing at the old dock and pump house in the distance. There was old mixed in with some new. He could see a very well preserved barbeque. He was hungry and visualized the burgers that he sometimes ate in cells. The cops never fed drunks as a rule. Once in awhile, there would be extra and the old cop would give one to him.

Ernie wasn't sure if he liked the old cop. He had stripes on his shoulder. Ernie knew enough about stripes from the Rangers. Some stripes meant he was more important than "no stripes" at all. No one gave the Rolicking street group any food. It simply didn't happen. They would have to normally seek out something edible in dumpsters. Ernie could not get over the garbage that he saw—perfectly good food. Once he found half of a chocolate bar. He remembered thinking at the time that it must be from a white kid or something. Why would anyone throw out a perfectly good chocolate bar?

The old trapper had learned not to try and make too much sense out of something so good. Ernie believed in his "keeper." There was someone who always looked after him.

The old trapper walked over to the wood shed. There was tons of wood—he would be okay at night. Hungry was one thing, cold and hungry all together different. His rib hurt when he was cold. He looked down at the key ring and walked over to another shed to try an old brass key. He opened the padlock and went inside. There were tools everywhere and an old 12 gauge leaned on a rusted table saw. Ernie picked up the gun and pushed the safety. He pulled the pump action. It was horribly stiff.

Ernie was mad and hated the fact that any weapon would be mistreated. A 12 gauge was a fine tool. It was not something to be left in a cold shed. Ernie grabbed the shotgun and a small can of oil. There was a canvas backpack hanging behind some poly water pipe. He rummaged through the backpack and found an old wide mouthed tartan colored thermos bottle. Once Ernie saw the old thermos, he remembered his youth in Wandering Lake. His grandfather would often take him trapping. The old wide mouth thermos would always be filled with caribou meat soup. Ernie shook his head and snapped back to reality. Thinking of food and distant memories would only make his hunger worse. He peered around the backpack and found an old bag of peanuts and a juice box, very good. He would eat the peanuts slowly.

His attention was drawn towards the next cabin. It was brown half logs with a large deck that ran around it. It was like a castle. This cabin had black iron grates across the windows. Smart guy, Ernie thought to himself. The old trapper knew he could break in from under the cabin, but it would make a lot of noise. There was really no reason. He had enough food for now. The old trapper felt that he was staying in a friendly place. He still wanted to look at the small buildings by the dock, but it would be too risky. He had taken a chance venturing out to the tool shed. The trip had been worth it.

Ernie went back around to the cabin and in through the same door. He saw a "boogie board" behind the old couch in the porch. It was blue and very bright against the black autumn sky. The old trapper had never played in the water. He had fished and hauled nets but he had never played. He wondered what it would be like to just hang out in a lake or a pool. The trapper saw rich folks do that on T.V. It always looked so damn dull. He opened the inner screen door to the main cabin and sat on the couch while leaning his body on the armrest. For some reason, it was always easier to breath sitting up.

His legs were restless, he could not sit still. He shuffled over to the bar and looked around the multitude of little shot glasses. The glasses were dusty and were captioned with little sayings. There was a myriad of shot, rocks, wine and martini glasses. Ernie got down while leaning sideways and peered down into the lower shelf. His eyes revealed a whiskey bottle, the kind with a handle. It had duct tape wrapped around the lid. The bottle was about half full. The sight of the bottle brought about a conflicting feeling of uneasy resolve. Drinking in the bush was not the norm. Liquor was not taken on the trap line. It wasn't so much the issue of drinking. It was instead, and more appropriately; the issue of place. However, the Americans always told him that the booze could help the pain.

The old man walked over to the old wood stove. It said "Selkirk" across the top. He was very familiar with this stove. It was big and charcoal grey with chrome colored twisted metal handles. There was a lighter on a small table and a small plastic box of old paper. The fire grew cautiously and it flickered slowly in the hearth. There wasn't any air intake on the old stove, so he tinkered with the chimney flue. There was a faint wind now. The smoke rose slowly up, through the chimney and out into the dark. The trapper went into the porch and got a bigger chunk of wood. He tossed it into the stove. The sparks jumped up and he latched the iron door. It would take hours before the main part of the cabin was warm. The old trapper strolled around. He found himself intrigued with the kid's room. There was life in this bedroom. Not every place brought about a good feeling. It was the end result of lasting spirit. The posters of city rock stars on the wall clashed with the rustic warm feeling of the pine. The furniture was old and the bed was 50's small. It looked more like a bunk in cells than a proper bed. It had a bright pink bedspread on it with fairies or something. The mystical people had seemingly, been conjured up from an opposing world.

The old trapper had no education in the world of fiction. His life existed in the stark reality of the present. Childhood was nothing but a shuffle from foster home to foster home. At ten years old his mother died. His father was last seen in Winnipeg—he had simply lost touch. Mother always kept the family together. She hated liquor of all types and would not tolerate it. It was a long time ago, the first time he came home drunk—he was nine. It was at a friend's house and there was a case of small mickey bottles in the kitchen. So he helped himself. Back then it only took one bottle. No one really noticed at the time. It was all about the moment. His mother never beat him until that day he came home drunk. Ernie brought his hand to his cheek and remembered the feeling of her warm hard hand striking his once smooth face. He realized now that there is often great love in the adult knowledge associated with a preemptive blow. The rage in her eyes was not the mother he knew so well. The blow hit much harder than mere force.

When his Mother died, the workers came. They would never leave him alone. In total there were six foster families; two in Bliss Landing and four in Rolicking. At an early age, he learned that if he ended up in cells, the social workers would be called. The choice to eventually give them up was made out of a greater sense of self evolution than adolescent need. Life on the streets began at the ripe old age of 14. He began the path not, out of an obstinate sense of teenage challenge but, out of decreed societal demand. Life in the bush was always best. Ernie relished in odd jobs like pumping fuel. Sometimes he wished he could do more with his life. He tried at the beginning to find work. There would be guiding work sometimes at Balding Lodge.

Balding Lodge was an outpost fishing camp that catered to wealthy Americans. They didn't seem to care that Ernie was Aboriginal. He knew where to fish and how to catch them. They would give him American money and he would feel good for a very brief time. Often he would leave the lodge with thousands of dollars. He would roll the money into a big roll and fasten it with an elastic band. There would be gifts for the group and they all would drink. They would buy real food if they were allowed into the restaurants. This was very hard because most of the time they had no money. When they had money they would go to the back door of "Rolicking Burgers." They would have to show the money in advance to the owner. It would cost maybe $50.00 for six burgers but it was worth every cent. No one cared as long as they didn't come in the restaurant. The group knew never to push things. The restaurant was warm but the stares from the whites' weren't worth it. Better off eating in the alley, it wasn't that bad.

It doesn't matter what things cost as long as you can spend. Ernie didn't really get prices. You either could buy something, or you could not. The owners at the lodge offered to save some of the guiding money for him. The old trapper knew he should have taken their advice but what would he save for…? If he could buy something now, it made much more sense to enjoy it.

Ernie reached into the deep jacket pocket and opened up the peanut bag. He took one out and savored it, "Dry Roasted" it said on the label. The trapper could read and he felt good about that… He did get enough schooling to learn how to write and sign his name on the prisoner sheets. It was only because his Mother had helped him—he felt blessed. Anything else that really mattered was taught to him by his mother and grandfather.

The cabin was getting warmer. Ernie had not yet touched the whiskey. He carefully unraveled the duct tape and drank from the bottle. He hated the way he drank from the bottle. He had seen movies with ice buckets and fancy glasses. He put the bottle down on the coffee table. He went around the bar and picked up a glass mug. It was all twisted up funny and bent up. It said on the side, "I got smashed in Rolicking City." Ernie giggled to himself and poured the glass full. His rib felt much better and he closed his eyes briefly. He woke up right away and reached over to the old Enfield. He kept it close—it always would be.

Chapter 11
Hill Mountain Co-op

Earl and Kate approached the small village of Hill Mountain. There wasn't much to this "one moose" town. As the duo entered the village there was the obligatory gas bar and restaurant on the west side. There was also the classic northern gift shop. You know, the kind of store that has just about everything Christmas for sale. On the east side and just about out of the town, was the Hill Mountain Co-op. The store was an old fishing enterprise from back at the turn of the century. Well, the old turn of the century, not the millennium. If you could not find it at the Co-op, it was not to be found anywhere in the North. The duo parked the Crown Vic out front of the store. It was a little early, almost 9:00 A.M.

Kate commented, "Great, the lights are still out. I called McIvor yesterday and told him we'd be here."

Earl replied, "Let's check out the coffee shop." Earl could not help but think about Superintendent Thompson. He wondered what kind of management bobbles he would be juggling right about now. The super's office in Bliss would naturally be pristine, not a shred of paper anywhere. You would think that they would at least try and mess things up a little! Why wouldn't any boss want to create the illusion of work? Fuck, even if you didn't have squat to do why not prop things up a little?

The door to the coffee shop had a ripped screen. It was a 60's dated ugly aluminum color. There was some sort of old motif on the metal work covering the old screen. It looked like the wings of a gryphon sporting the tits of a stripper. The door opened outwards accompanied with the classic horror movie screech. The resulting noise was the by-product of rusted hinges dragging on bare metal. The inner door was wide open. The coffee shop was a classic look, almost retro but in reality, far too dumpy and beat up by discerning retro standards. Kate and Earl took a seat in the booth to the far back. There were two truckers seated at the lunch counter. Kate and Earl made no effort to hide their issued "chunks." Their sidearm's clung to their respective hips. In theory, a cop was supposed to keep a gun covered up and out of sight. In practice, no one at least in the North, really cared.

Earl leaned over to Kate, "What ya having babe?"

Kate replied, "Well, I should have some oatmeal but how would that look?"

Earl popped back, "No point getting bunged up on my account. Eat what the hell ya want."

* * * *

Kate looked around the coffee shop. There was no effort here to brighten things up. The business only existed for the truck traffic and tourists in the summer. Most of the tourists are long gone come October. Kate noticed the large clock on the wall. It had an off white face with ugly yellow green luminescent hands. There was an old "bee bop" hula girl in the middle of the clock. Her hands rotated around the clock face. When the clock struck twelve, the grass skirt came down. The icon had been there for years.

The oriental family that ran the restaurant knew that for one reason or another, the truckers poured in at 11:50 A.M. All heads awkwardly cranked up for the skirt show at noon. It wasn't really the issue of the skirt. Let's face it, if you wanted porn you could see far more skin than the clock could provide! It had simply become the intangible gimmick that brought in the customers. The food was actually half decent—it had to be. If the food wasn't good, the truckers would simply hold out for their final destination.

Kate noticed one of the truckers at the counter. He was a large man with keys that swung from a belt chain. He had a bulging wallet hanging from his back pocket. The wallet was noticeably oversized. His ass perched on the old stool like a dinosaur sitting on a mushroom. Kate thought to herself how damn uncomfortable it must be. She found herself looking at rear ends far too much lately. The back side formed the benchmark of her ongoing self critique. She was at that age where her body had changed faster than her ability to accept change. It wasn't like the detective didn't watch what she ate. It was more a matter of watching it go in her mouth. Buns she thought buns....

Earl leaned over, "Don't worry I won't let you down. I'm having a cinnamon number! I'm even going to sop it in gobs of butter. What do you think about that…?"

Kate laughed the morning was all about self indulgence. It was impossible to diet on the road. In spite of her good intentions, the calorie counter didn't play out well with Earl.

* * * *

The old owner who was only known around town as "Mom" hovered around them. "How are you two cops doing today?" Mom's old teeth smiled with the total sincerity of a long abandoned dental plan. Bits of black and yellow teeth caught the reflecting morning light. Her face evoked substantial character—there wasn't an ounce of pretense in her body.

Earl replied, "Ma, we be doing just great! Have you seen Jason around?"

Mom looked down and said, "Do I fucking look like Jason's keeper?" She explained herself in the least amount of detail possible. She elaborated, "Grown man … do what the hell he wants!"

Earl knew this was going nowhere fast and upped the anti, "I'll have one of your classic cinnamon buns and the lady wants some oatmeal."

Mom never missed a Chinese beat, "She no lady—she's a cop." Mom immediately chuckled, turned away from Earl and then smiled ear to ear at Kate. She held the white pad out front, "Only instant oatmeal, that okay…?"

Kate replied, "Okay, I give—I'll have a bun too." She felt the need to rationalize the switch in culinary sentiment. Earl just stared. He knew that Kate would break before he would. Kate looked at Earl and then Earl "returned face" at Kate. It wasn't the "Coral" gaze he got on the way up. It was instead, the "Okay … I know I'm fat but you must shut the fuck up look." Kate wondered what the hell is he doing. Finally, she could not hold it in any longer and exclaimed, "Okay I'm fat, you happy now, so I'm having a god damn bun!"

Earl noticed that much like a cartoon character, Mom's eyebrow swerved up when she spoke. She sported a once classic white apron, spotted with just the right amount of character invoking grease. The apron had large pockets at the waist. It was the quintessential cross between a Carpenter's apron and a Ferrier's smock. The old staff felt he was doing real well. Kate would expect the typical counter jab but he would stick handle around it.

He dramatically broke the silence and the gawk, "Looks like a damn fine day!" Kate looked on in total disbelief. It was really too early for this stuff. He looked down at the paper place mat which had the various corporate sponsors printed along the border. There was everything from Rocker's Real Estate to Pavlov's Pet Supplies.

Earl said, "I'm going to the boy's room." He was proud of himself. He really didn't have to go that bad but the most important thing was the proverbial *cue*. Earl had cued up Kate and, an exit stage right was automatically demanded. A well executed cue was considered right up there with the slip. The washrooms were right around the corner from the booth. Earl commenced his journey down the dark hall. He noticed the irregular flooring and chipped ceramic tiles. If a customer felt like they were walking on a slant, it was simply because the floor was fucking crooked. There was that subtle ambiance associated with the very strange smell of urine combined with the aroma of cinnamon buns. Earl remarked to himself just how well the baking covered up the stink. Maybe that's what the office needed rounding second by the ladies washroom.

He wondered if Mom was even remotely aware of the smell. Of course, no one would care until Jenn, the Health Inspector, made her rounds. Mom didn't mind either if she got shut down in October. It was far better than during the summer. In reality, it was a safe bet. There would probably be few visits from provincial officials during the summer.

Earl opened the "Boy's Room" door. It hung from one hinge and brown rust was painted everywhere. Only the survey lines drawn in imagination could separate the corner lot of rust and shit. The toilet had the northern issue scum and "whatever" stains all over it. Most folks knew that they likely wouldn't die at the hands of "whatever" germs." The trouble was, it still looked damn bad!

Earl noticed a foot long end of electrical heat tape wrapped around the sink drain. Nothing could be so reassuring to the defecating client. Complementing the picture, was an off-white toilet seat that moved freely on the bowl. Earl tossed up the old seat to the "male number one" attack position. He questioned his logic for a minute, shrugged and slammed it back down hard. It seemed strangely out of place not to piss all over the seat. Earl took his time while taking precise aim and picked off a good portion of the decaying seat. The goal of the strategic exercise was to best avoid destructive blow back. Out of a greater sense of consciousness—he washed his hands. As expected, there was only a trickle of cold water. Come winter, the trickle would be reduced to drops as the pipes froze up. Double checking his fly, Earl straightened himself while exiting the washroom. He slowly waltzed down the hall and returned to the booth.

* * * *

Kate perused the investigational file. She looked over the details of the robbery at the Co-op. It was about two weeks old now. There were no surveillance cameras in the store. A lone guy had walked in early in the A.M. According to McIvor, the suspect pointed a gun at him and demanded money from the till. Mostly taken were lottery tickets and some liquor. The Co-op had a government liquor store in the back. It was nothing much but it stocked the essential beverages of life. There was no mention in the file as to lottery ticket lot number or the type of liquor taken. Kate hated this stuff. Questions that seemed so obvious to her were always left out of investigations. Kate scribbled down some rough interview notes. She would record the statement in the essence of time. Clues were long gone but she hoped to clarify those all too frequent, dead ends.

Mom came over to the booth with cinnamon buns in tow. "You want butter?"

Earl replied, "Abso-loutely."

Kate looked down at the mammoth bun and her only thoughts were, fucking fat wielding opponent from hell. As if tactically positioned, the nuts and syrup clung enticingly to the dough. Kate really didn't want to eat the bun. She convinced herself, consistent with the time of the month, that all cravings must be satisfied. The buns were hot, in fact much hotter than the coffee. One of the truckers came around the counter and grabbed the coffee pot. He filled up his cup, his trucking partners and then walked down to the "police" booth. He didn't say a word to the duo and nodded while topping up their cups.

Earl looked up, "That's awful nice of you. Thanks very much!"

The big trucker acknowledged politely. Kate thought to herself how nice the trucker was. First impressions sometimes do suck. Kate looked at the warm cinnamon bun and it smelled damn good. She picked off a couple of the hazelnuts and fired them in her mouth. The detective had a lifelong penchant for sweets. She watched the trucker slowly stroll down the aisle and she, once again, noticed the fat wallet. She found it amazing that the wallet could remain in his pocket. It was like there was Velcro on the trucker's ass or something.

* * * *

Earl looked at the clock, "Not quite show time but certainly time to check out the Co-op." Earl didn't wait for the bill he just fired $10.00 on the table. He knew that was plenty. They exited the coffee shop and the morning sun was warm now. Earl took a minute and put on his shades. They weren't designers like the kid cops. They were Rolik-Mart "clip on" more befitting his seniority. The air brakes of another rig tossed some racket into the morning air. They walked down a couple of the broken wooden stairs and across the gravel driveway. Once again, they banged on the door to the Co-op.

"Still not open?" Earl questioned. There was no home address. Possibly, he lived in back of the store. Earl peered through the store window. He positioned himself in the hooker position, wiped off some window grime with his sleeve and peered in the store.

Kate opened her cell phone out of reflex, "God damn it. No cell service in Hill Mountain—knew that...."

Earl walked around the back of the Co-op. There was a black mutt on a chain that growled at him. It wasn't a biker dog or anything like that. The staff noticed that the right front paw was bleeding. There were some other blood patterns around the back. At the rear of the store there was an old white door slightly ajar. It was about two feet off the ground. The steps to the door had long since vanished or decayed.

In his best high pitched girly voice, Earl tried to calm the dog down. The dog looked at him and must have "doggie sensed" that he was in the midst of a "good shit." He petted the dog while evaluating the exterior and surrounding yard. There wasn't much in the back but garbage, a derelict old truck and the hull of a broken tri-hull boat. There was also a bit of a well trampled bush path that vanished into the tree line. Earl walked around the dog and picked up a stick. He pushed on the door. Surprisingly, it did not swing open immediately. The old staff stretched up and leaned his full weight on the door. The dog looked up and cocked his head in disapproval while Kate spun around the corner.

Earl quickly hollered, "Go back to the front, the door is open. I'm going to try and get inside. Check out the blood out back." The old staff continued to shove at the door and pushed carefully with his right shoulder causing several boxes to tumble. Earl was no track star yet he wasn't exactly ready for the "home" either. He peeked through the crack of the door. He hollered, "Mr. McIvor, Rolicking Police." There was no sound, he regrouped and went back to the front of the store to meet Kate. Earl detailed the situation while employing a phony "formal" voice.

Earl stated, "I think we have a situation."

At the time, Kate could not have agreed less. Sure, there was blood but the dog had a hurt paw. Kate was also very conscious of her current "garb." The pant suit wasn't "haute couture" but it sure wasn't a Hill Mountain jumper either! She was losing her patience, "For fucks sakes let's just get going, we can try again on the way back."

Earl knew that on face value, there was little here, but he was cop bugged. It was the kind of "bug" that he always got when something was not quite right. Earl said, "I can't help it ... I'm going to try and get in the store through the back. Hang tough in the front." Earl retraced his steps and took a closer look at the terrain. There had not been rain for quite some time. The rocky dirt was bone dry. Interesting or not, there was some motor oil on the ground not far from the dog. Earl looked to the distance. There was open field for 100 feet then the tree line started.

The dog was fine now. The animal appeared almost reassured and calm around Earl. With the utmost disregard for process and civil rights, the old staff decided to go into the store. He found a good sized chunk of lumber in the wood pile and swung it like he was taking down a tree. A couple more boxes crashed to the floor. Earl stepped up to the plate and into the store. The floor boards creaked as Earl slowly entered—it was still very dark. The distinct smell of rotting, moldy lumber engulfed the air. He could barely see the front window through the doorway into the main store.

All that Earl could think about was that Kate would see his shadow and shoot him. They had no portable radios and the cells were useless. There was an old rotary dial phone hanging from the wall. Earl picked up the receiver hoping to call the Telecom's Center. There was no dial tone. He removed his sidearm from the holster and crouched down while navigating through the array of stock boxes. He had no flashlight and he could not find the light switch. For a brief moment, Earl pondered, why the fuck didn't I go to Bliss solo?

The store was strangely familiar from the past. His prior visits without a gun consisted of buying cigarettes, chips and mix—the real staples of life. Once in awhile Judy would mail a letter or send a package. The little postal outlet was handy in the summer. When the kids were younger this was the ice cream shack. It didn't seem much like an ice cream shack now. The old staff made his way to the light. Upon approaching the doorway, he realized that the rear of the store was separated by two swinging doors. There were round windows on each door and a big gap of sunlight filtered between them. One of the round windows had no glass at all.

The same *Mom type* piss smell invaded Earl's nose. He looked down at his dress pants which were now dusty around the knees. Earl exited the stock room area and found himself in the main store. He noticed that several cans were strewn from the shelves. He walked to the front of the store and opened the main door to let Kate in.

Once Kate was in, she walked to the cash and opened the till. There was cash and a couple of checks. She wondered why the hell Jason hadn't emptied the till the night before? Earl went up and down the aisles. There was a freezer sitting on the floor with some ice cream and popsicles. It was the same chest freezer that the kids always dived into when they were younger. Along the north wall were two other upright refrigerated coolers.

Earl hovered outside the cooler door and looked up at the stock. He noticed there was the usual assortment of pop, milk, juice and one old container of almost ready baking dough. In addition, there were cheese slices, chip dip, bologna, whipped cream and a hand. Earl swung his head mechanically back and directly in line with the position of the hand. The old staff looked intriguingly at the inanimate object. The hand was lying fingers down as if it had somehow crawled there itself. The cooler doors were iced over from condensation build up. It was hard to see clearly. It was a left hand and there was a bronze colored ring on the pinky finger. Earl continued to stare and shouted out, "Kate, do you see a right hand anywhere?"

Kate replied, "What the fuck?"

Earl turned to face Kate, "You know those kid's books, what does not fit the picture? What does not belong? You wanna play, well do you?" Earl took a bag of peanuts from a rack and tore open the top.

* * * *

Kate gawked at the cooler and then back to Earl. She found herself not nearly as riled as she should have been.

Earl said, "Look way down and I'll call Rusty!"

Kate squinted and refocused her eyes. Her line of sight caught the hand but she took no notice of the ring. The detective could only see bits of hair and languid looking meat hanging from what was once, a wrist. Kate, felt her "cinnamon bun" pulling at her gut. It very clearly, wanted to spasm out an air borne exit. Kate stepped back from the cooler and her stomach quickly calmed down. It wasn't so much the hand. Kate had seen her share of blood. More aptly, it was the *venue of display*. Kate had seen it all but she wasn't ready for everything evil at 10:00 A.M. in the morning!

She turned to the old one, "Why the fuck didn't you warn me? You sick twisted asshole."

* * * *

Earl fired a peanut in his mouth and replied, "You think I'm twisted: how 'bout the guy that did the manicure." He left the store and walked over to the cruiser. "RCP, Rogers, Rolicking!" bellowed Earl into the microphone.

A voice replied, "Go ahead Staff…."

Earl started to say, "We are in Hill Mountain right now and we need a ha … n'd ." Earl slammed the vocals hard and regrouped, "Rolicking, I'm going to call this in from a land line." Earl walked back into the store. He said, "I'm going to Mom's to use their phone in case the bad guys used McIvor's phone. What do you think detective? Does it look like McIvor's hand? Oh ya, if you got some police tape maybe you could tie one end to the hand and wrap the other end around the cooler."

Earl strolled out of the Co-op and back into Mom's. He asked Mom to use the phone and was motioned by a wave to the far wall by the cash. There was no one in the restaurant now. Earl dialed Rolicking, he was strangely very conscious of the *life like action* of his dialing digit. The dial phone brought back images of his youth. It really did take way longer to dial. He spoke with Gretchen and they exchanged Earl's version of an update.

He informed Gretchen in his best staff voice, "We are in Hill Mountain and I need the crew from ICU up here with Ident. Mushy wouldn't hurt either. Oh ya, would you please call Thompson and tell him I'm tied up and won't make our appointment."

Gretchen yelled into the receiver, "Have you lost it Earl? You have to go or the boss will flip out!"

Earl replied, "Yes, I have lost it and need to find its owner."

Gretchen sensed the immediate change in tone, "Not another one...?"

Earl clarified, "It's hard to tell at this point, we got a hand in a cooler, blood and squat. One thing for sure, someone left the hand on display and that worries me a little." He hung up the phone and thought to himself why anyone would leave a hand in a cooler? Beside the whipped cream, no less! The culprit is guilty of both bad taste and unconventional littering. Certainly, there must be an infraction under the Health Act. The old staff shrugged and headed back to the Co-op. Earl looked out the window from Mom's. It was now almost "game time." In a matter of hours the place would be crawling with cops and news people. Evidence is never easy to manage at the best of times. Increased frenzy in a small town almost always equaled issues.

Earl glanced at his watch. He was grateful that there was no cell service in Hill Mountain or the damn sir would have called him by now. He lit up a smoke as he walked back to Kate, "It really isn't that great of a morning after all. Is it?"

Kate looked at her colleague with the eyes of someone much older, "I'm just getting beat up Earl, the human body wasn't made to absorb this much grief."

For a brief second Earl found himself strangely empathetic with Kate's comments. Introspective analysis was not something that came easily to Earl. He was not typically a deep thinker, or was he? If the lake was only four feet shallow than was it really deep? Trees almost always fell in the Manitoba forest, but they are puny and abundant—does it really matter if anyone hears? There was something about Kate's grief comment that forced the old one to dig deep into his suit pocket. He counted two more T3's and he fired one in his mouth like a peanut. Kate stared off across the road. There was nothing to look at. Their collective job at this point was to secure the scene until the troops come from Rolicking. Something of this magnitude, with possible linkages to the other murder, would require concerted investigation. Earl hoped that the troops coming from Rolicking would bring some decent groceries. It seemed to Earl, like he often forgot the most important elements of crime scene management. This included but was not limited to gitch, socks, coffee, chips, mix, something to augment the mix, paper, pens, laptops, overtime forms and something to augment the mix.

You could easily expect to be at any crime scene for 48 hours, sometimes less but generally speaking a couple of days. It had almost become necessary to spend two days because of perception. Nowadays, less than two days left a jaded sense of perception that the cops didn't really care. Nothing could be further from the truth. Often very complex killings only give up a small amount of forensic evidence. Once the evidence was examined and in the "mix" the only point of staying was for show value. This logic of course, only pertains to a police perspective, politics always played the lead. This scene would be no different. Earl accepted the fact that the show must have the curtain up for 48 hours.

There was a time when Earl could not get enough of the "gravy train" but now he found himself in the position of chief engineer. The gravy train was the cop cash cow that always came about from someone else's tragedy. The metaphoric train also referred to the process of investigation. How well that train rode or derailed would be placed squarely on Earl's shoulders. Kate was his ally in crime. She was the super sleuth and Earl was the "manager in charge" of invoicing the cape and tights. There were times when the old staff just wanted to go back to being a constable on ICU. Life was super good back then. You fired in an overtime claim and harassed the piss out of the boss until it was signed. Crime fighting 20 years ago was street sport. The cost involved or resulting blow back was always shielded by the man in charge.

Kate turned to Earl, "Listen I'd better park around back just to say we did ... in case there is some activity."

Earl replied, "You can go but don't drive the PC around until Ident gets there. Tell you what, I'll buy joe and cigarettes if you can manage the dash over to Mom's."

Kate said, "If you go then I'll buy—we need cigarettes, coffee and some pads."

Earl gave the detective some major glare back and he took out his notebook. His pen came out like a waiter at a diner. His hand travelled the longer 180 degree route from the sports coat pocket to the front of the notebook. Earl said, "Kate you got caught again with your pants down on the job?"

"That's the problem, damn gun, damn rags, damn boys all around me that don't have any of these fucking problems."

In a very "ultra modern" fashion, Earl lifted one brow and clarified, "I've bought pads before, no issues—green box or red? Any guy will tell you that, for some reason, it's almost always the green box."

Kate replied, "The generic yellow on black *Mom's pads* will do just fine." She grabbed at the cigarette pack that Earl had fired in his suit pocket. Kate didn't feel like a smoker but there were times at work or under the influence of significant cocktails, that a butt just completed the unsavory picture. She felt fidgety and restless. It was overwhelming desperate tension that greater fueled the problem. Cigarettes at crime scenes fit well in the old detective movies but in the DNA age—not a great plan. Kate swung away from the steps. She grabbed an old tin can from the street garbage to catch the ashes. No point starting a fire.

Earl didn't really want to go back to Mom's. It wasn't because of distance. He just felt that he should be hanging with Kate. Earl knew in his heart of hearts that he was on a very noble mission. The most important acts of policing do not come with medals. There had been a standing joke around the office that you could judge a murder by Kate's cycle. In fact, the troops took it so much to heart that they actually bought on credit under the presumption that certain evil would necessarily happen. The troops were told to shut up about their speculation. Typically, spouses planned around their "cop partners" working late while they devoured the online shopping sites.

The North had become a hot bed of criminal activity. It was just too damn big and the combination of alcohol, drugs and money—virtually insurmountable. Earl manipulated his hand to his ear and listened for the sirens in the distance. There was really no reason for the emergency response but he knew that the young bucks could not resist the rising woody associated with sirens, bells and whistles.

Earl wondered to himself if he ever gave a damn about lights and sirens. It never seemed to matter back then. Maybe it was the video gaming of the 90's that had fostered a greater sense of action associated with the game of cops and robbers. Young cops just loved every single toy on a police car. The old staff knew nothing about video games. Of course, there was an old game of "pong" at the cabin which he fired up once in awhile. Earl could still remember the challenges of the 1/32" tennis paddle—now that was live action!

Earl tugged on the screen door. The restaurant was still empty. There was an area behind the cash that displayed the basic necessities of life. There were several toothbrushes, toothpaste, mouthwash, Rolaids, Kleenex and believe it or not ribbed condoms. Earl shook his head, in a world of ribbed condoms behind the cash, I see no fucking pads!

Without missing a mental beat, Earl surfed into Mom's world, "Mom, you got any pads?"

"What you mean pads, SOS? You want more cinnamon buns?"

"No what I mean are pads for women."

Like a price check at the drug store, Mom hollered back, "Oh, sanitary napkins!"

Earl now in far too deep, "Yes!"

Mom stared at him and jabbed back, "No." Mom kept the glare on just like Kate in the cruiser. She promptly dropped her stare and said, "You good man!" Earl ordered one normal coffee and one jazzed up coffee to go. He also scored an extra pack of smokes. On his way out Mom casually enquired, "Where is Mr. Mike?"

Earl clarified, "You mean Sergeant Funk?"

Mom, "Ya, that's the guy. I have not seen him this week."

Earl shrugged it off. It didn't make much sense but in all fairness to Mom, she never made much sense. She was a good soul and very hard working. Much like Jean at the hardware store, there were people in this world that worked too damn hard and there were those that always dragged their asses. The trouble was, the "ass draggers" seemed to be winning out. Earl hated that with a passion. He opened the door with his shoulder while juggling the two coffees. The T3 was starting to take the edge off things. The headaches were getting much worse. He was a victim of his own coping mechanisms. Like most old cops the will to work didn't die off—it was the body that eventually hacked the line.

Earl walked back to Kate. The cigarette that hung in his mouth was now reduced to a painfully small smoldering butt. Kate was standing on the front ledge of the store. Earl casually looked around the back as he came from Mom's. Things were real quiet now. Once in awhile the crew could hear the banging of dump trucks to the North end of town. There were several quarries in town that fed the steady diet of highways work for the province. Earl stared at Kate and with all the sincerity he could muster said, "Solly, no pads."

Kate was kind of set back. She really didn't expect Earl to ask Mom. She was impressed that he had. Some guys give chocolates, some guys give flowers and Earl just gave the gift of no pads.

Chapter 12
The Exhibit Locker

P.B. sat outside the Department's exhibit locker. There was a computer situated in the doorway immediately beside him. A computer program called "Exhibit Zip" (EZ) was now utilized by the Department in order to track an exhibit from initial seizure, storage, processing and finally through the court process. The program came along with a bar coding scanner and stickers. Pretty much just like the food store.

Mike Funk was the regular Exhibit Custodian but he was off duty now, well allegedly "LL." Earl really had no one to saddle with the daily grind of moving exhibits seized by the troops. The effort consisted of an assembly line of constantly seized goods and chattels. The rule book dictated that a senior officer was required to move an article from an overnight Watch locker into the main exhibit locker.

P.B. had enough years under his belt to know that it really mattered how exhibits were handled. Once seized by an officer, a gun, bullet, DNA sampling, sex kit or statement had to be moved from the officer's overnight locker and into the main locker. For court purposes, a chain of continuity had to be established that could not be broken.

P.B. could remember the time he got caught off guard in court. He had entered some stolen VHS video tapes on the system, but he couldn't find a box to cyber check "video." There was a check off box for television, radio, construction equipment, bodily sample, paper document but squat for videotape. There was clearly no other option. He tried to bypass EZ but the system would only hurdle back red error messages. Finally, he just entered the category "DVD." EZ was happy now, it turned green and the world that day—was a much happier place. As things turned out, the system generated a court report with a time line that reflected "DVD" and not "VHS video." The problem was, the word "video" was contained in no less than 46 boxes on the printed time line. It is one thing to make a single error in policing and quite another to have that error reflected 46 times! The Crown Attorney had a fit and she settled for a plea.

No one liked doing the exhibit daily chore. Mike Funk, as the Operational Sergeant, was stuck with it. P.B. was subsequently thrown the reputed bone by Kate and Earl. He could hear Earl's words now, "You want that big job in Bliss. Here is what management work is really all about!" There was an overnight exhibit locker for each RCP Watch. He would take each exhibit one by one. He didn't want to spend too much time in the main locker or he would have to suit up. The fumes from the chemical dope like crystal meth would catch up to a guy. He had known some officers that even tried to spend quality absorption time in the main locker simply for, the "buzz factor."

The walls of the exhibit locker were painted a stark eggshell white color. This is the same bleak white color which adorned just about every house in Rolicking. The shelves were a wonderful puke green Government Issue color. There were rows and rows of shelves and plastic containers. The plastic containers held everything from dope and guns to assorted electronic gadgetry. There were also the "people pieces" accompanied logically, by fluids taken from people. These samples lived in a dedicated cooler unit. There are some things in life which you should never accidently mix, body parts is one of them.

The walls were laden down with gun racks hosting beat up guns. Most of the old rifles were enshrouded with hockey and electrical tape. A Rolicking Saturday night special most often consisted of a pipe with a nail for a hammer which, was in turn, activated by a pull spring. There were all kinds of street toys in the exhibit locker which included but were not limited to .22 single shot pens, .22 cell phone guns and even .22 dildo launchers. It goes without saying that a guy's .308 is in reality, a chick's .22. The arsenal housed every conceivable multiple shot weapon known to man. There were even assorted "low tech" archery kits and crossbows. The detective could not remember the last time that a valiant knight died at the hands of a crossbow. He shrugged to himself while thinking; it might work. Guess you wouldn't hear the arrow coming. There were bolt, lever, pump actions and everything in between. For a Northern locker it even housed its share of advanced automatic weaponry. P.B.

wondered if the inventor of the Uzi could have ever imagined its final resting place. Most of these weapons would either be saved for court or destroyed locally under the watching eye of a senior manager.

One side of the exhibit locker was exclusively filled with firearms. The other side housed evidence relating to cold homicide investigations. Whether it was from a recent, a 20 year old dead homicide or a hot case, the Department was obligated to retain the snotty tissue. Heaven forbid you didn't because the old snotty tissue from circa 1970 now represented possible salvation for the guilty. It's understandable if the person was actually "not guilty" but to be sprung because of a police failure to retain snot—a very far reach. "Reverse onus" had now been taken to mean that the cops had to fully validate historical conviction.

P.B. stared at the sea of exhibits. Sooner or later the Department would need a warehouse in Bolivia! At one time there were also liquor exhibits everywhere. Now the cops just dumped the stuff. He shrugged as he thought to himself about his current job, "Was he well on his way to "Earl'dom?" He respected the old staff but that didn't mean they always saw eye to eye. P.B. knew that he needed Earl's good favor in order to elicit solid comments on his promotion docs. The Vindication exercise meant nothing, without the strong and fully documented support from the man in charge. A promotional Vindication meant squat from the candidate unless it was supported in spades.

Everyone knew that the superintendent hated the staff with a passion but there was virtually nothing he could do to quash Earl's comments. Opinions still mattered in the process. They were especially important to the Bliss Landing Police Association. More than one grievance had been won based on supervisory perceptions or negative comments that could not be validated. Earl had the gift of the gab and an often misunderstood, sense of the pen. His superiors and the politicians in town had learned that the hard way. Much like that old "B Movie" cop in the rain coat, Earl had the knack of being able to dupe his opponents into believing he was "damn dumb." The old staff was smart enough to realize that his edge would always remain in his inherent ability to work the con.

Each time an exhibit went out for court or the lab it would be initialed by the officer. In and out movement would be cyber tracked. Each and every facet of exhibit processing had been detailed in the system. It was a well known fact that human error most often accounted for processing problems. Of course, humans still worked the system. There were no fail safes. There was "in theory" no way that an exhibit could move in or out of the cement fortress without EZ winking an eye of approval.

The locker was by anyone's stretch of the imagination, a fucking dump. The old staff had always threatened to clean it up and Funk had always fired back a reason for keeping it messy. One thing for sure, P.B. was not going to clean this up in any short order. He resigned himself to the drudgery of the game until the next big crisis hit ICU. Someone always got stuck with the exhibit job. Typically, this was flung on Kate but she was smart enough to be tied up. The only salvation would be a call to a greater calamity. Of course, this would typically generate even more exhibits.

The Department had tried to hire a civilian to manage the mess but there were always money problems. Most things better came with a price tag that never seemed to surpass the political hurdle. It makes much more sense tying up a cop that makes $70,000 then hiring an old boy or girl for $40,000. Logic never plays a big part in politics—money always does. P.B. regrouped his rambling thoughts and focused on exhibit processing. He went over to the "A" Watch overnight locker and picked up a seized rifle, a .308 bolt action. He surfed into EZ and hashed out the file number. He noted the date and time the gun went into the main locker. He peeled off a bar code sticker from the sheet of ten.

Strangely, the .308 was actually a very nice weapon. The stock was in mint condition. P.B. smiled and stuck the sticker on the beautiful maple stock— there that'll teach the bastard! If the court gives him back the gun, he'll never get the sticker off without wrecking the finish. If the glue used on the back side of police stickers could only be bottled P.B. would quit the Department. A cop would never do this if the gun was seized from a decent person. In this case, the weapon was taken from a group of fat ass hunters that were caught poaching. In P.B.'s mind, this type of player was always fair game.

It was so easy to put the exhibits in the locker and quite another story to find them again. P.B. looked up and down the wall of weaponry. He took an old .12 gauge pump down while placing the vastly improved and much better looking lever action in the racks. The nice guns got top billing and the beat up ones hit the peanut gallery. Suffice to state, that the guns in the racks represented the best of the worst. It didn't take that much of a cut to make the RCP top billing. It just required the obvious absence of hockey tape and super glue!

Once the gun was in the rack then P.B. was required to painstakingly enter the location of the weapon. The racks were all numbered much like the shelves. There was nothing worse than trying to find an exhibit just before trial. It's not like exhibits walked away, but they did sometimes manage to crawl onto another shelf.

It was a scientific fact that the exhibit elves were known to scamper under the main exhibit locker door and move stuff around. No one knew where they lived or presumed motive but the elves were real. P.B. wanted to set up a camera in the locker and catch the little people at work. They must be damn strong. They had to be in very good shape to collectively move heavy objects from one shelf to another. One wrong entry in EZ and the whole process would be doomed! A miscue during a trial could result in legal rants heard far and wide. If large and valueless items were misplaced no biggie. If a kilo of cocaine was misplaced—a big deal.

The last of the four walls contained everything "sexy." The wall was shrouded in dildos, whips, plastic chains, latex gitch, one unicycle with a flat tire and one trapeze. There were also rows and rows of sealed RCP sex kits. Some of the older exhibits had countless initials all over them reflecting their volatile movement over the years.

Back in pervert corner, P.B. eyeballed the jiggling purple rubber. He remembered when Bush responded to a shoplifting at "Jugs Novelties." Suffice to state, that jugs referred to neither milk nor juice. Presumably, the customer was too embarrassed to buy a huge purple dildo and simply ran out the door. Bush caught the call and eventually found the guy, dildo in hand running down a gravel road. The vision brought a chuckle to P.B. It wasn't so much the dildo in hand thing but the conjured up vision of Bush's, "Stop police. Drop that rubber pecker!" Fuck the shit that is not caught on police video, is truly the hard core essence of policing.

Everywhere he looked there were memories of both good and fucked up files. There were even some records, the music kind, contained on shelf slot "E209." The sticker on one plastic container was dated 1963. P.B. at the ripe old age of 31' was never exposed to records. He found himself looking at the ginormity of the vinyl disk. How could such a large flat object produce quality sound? None of it made much sense.

P.B. moved on to the "C" Watch overnight locker. There was a wooden bat, one soccer cleat, an old red umbrella, a kitchen fryer and a golf club. Ironically, there was a good chance that everything was seized during the same investigation. P.B. mentally wandered into the realm of investigational possibilities while glancing at a kilo of cocaine wrapped up in plastic. Typically, in the wacky world of ICU, Kate or P.B. would necessarily be drawn into a seizure of that size. He surfed into the investigational file and it was a highway rip that was pipelined. Pipelining is the process of extreme fishing. You sit, you wait and you drink coffee until your prey falls victim. On the Manitoba highway, there are no such things as barbless hooks.

Pipelining bad guys is an acquired art form. Bush was the RCP's best. He was known to come in on his own time and just hang out at the edge of town. Of course, there were always subtle clues like a Corvette in the middle of winter or a pickup with a spoiler in the back! A pickup with a spoiler in the back always meant a solid rip! If only the owners of said, supped up wonder, knew that they would be immortalized on the pipeline "A" list!

P.B. walked over to the coke shelf and ensured that the exhibit was marked correctly. He went over to EZ and entered the shelf number "D314" which meant third drug shelf, section fourteen. The scanner could not scan everything. The third drug shelf was top billing. P.B. got up on a step stool to handle the exhibit. He noticed other coke exhibits in the same neighborhood area. There were several packages captioned with very well known local characters. The initials BTR stood out on one pack of coke. There was another bigger pack of coke with the same initials. P.B. had never met the officer one, Brendan Richards but he knew that he had long since quit the RCP. P.B. shrugged it off, the paper work must be awaiting disposition from Health Canada. In some cases, it could take years before the dope can be dumped! There were lots of drug exhibits in the locker pending the "Authority to Dispose." Sometimes the dope got sent back to Ottawa. Other times, the permission was granted to destroy the product locally.

The bottom line, no one would ever catch shit for having too many exhibits in the locker! The focus of management's attention was primarily activated when guns, dope or money went walking. For the collective value of shits and giggles, P.B. tried to query the old BTR exhibit. There were no outstanding exhibits. In all likelihood, this was because EZ was still an infant in the womb ten years ago. The exhibits at that point in time were all managed on paper. How dull that job must have been! Manually entering all this stuff with a pen would have certainly brought a grown man to tears.

P.B. was all for high tech investigational tools like "Computer Crime Scene Management" (CCSM). Computer management was essentially the "be all and end all" of crime fighting. These days, it wasn't so much the super cop flying through the air but the "MAP" (map and mouse) investigator. It wasn't so much that a computer could solve a real "who dunnit" but it was more about disciplined, turbo charged, mega watt wielding, roid' rage induced "systematized" organization. So many times the crime scene was all wrapped up before the cops did their thing. The crime scene happenings seduced you into believing a plausible story whereas cyber crime tools anchored the investigator to fact. The trouble with the element of fact is that it tends to be very malleable and more so than not, takes its final shape from the collateral renderings of storytelling.

P.B. was still in deep thought when Gretchen strolled into the locker. She was noticeably out of breath and stated, "You have been paroled. Earl called, he is with Kate and there is a scene at Hill Mountain. Something about a severed hand in the Co-op."

P.B. had grown accustomed to Earl's whimsy. He likely just needed some more pampering. The calls that ICU received were almost always embellished. If there was a call to a homicide with a flying saucer then absolutely no one would even lift a brow. Once there was a submarine sighting and the Department did up a press release. The inherent problem with the sighting was that it was at Shallow Lake. According to the RCP rule book, Ops II, Page 63; "Submarines most certainly require 36 feet of water...."

Gretchen clarified, "Earl wants you to bring Mushy and the scientists with you." Mushy was the Department's police dog handler.

The scientists were the "Forensic Identification Specialists." The dog handler was based in Rolicking but the scientists would have to come via District in Bliss Landing. Rolicking used to have a team of Ident but the cut backs of the 90's ended all that. The macro empire evolved in Bliss and now the scientists were on call virtually 24/7. They did nothing but drive and fly all over the North. Their job was so demanding that they now only attended priority calls. P.B. thought to himself that the superintendent would likely be attending Hill Mountain.

It was standard procedure. Ident would have to deploy because of the current political heat. With the numbers of dead bodies came resolve to find a killer. Always submitted for reflection, is the possibility that there was more than one killer. If something suspicious materialized in Hill Mountain, then that could mean the bad guy was branching out. P.B. speculated that he didn't know anyone that had used a serial killer example in a Vindication.

The troops always knew that it was never dull when Harold and Earl got together. There was the famous police dinner three years ago where Earl hurled a fully dressed baked potato at the superintendent. Harold was, post attack "all dressed" in full dress uniform. Nothing like sour cream, chives and bacon bits dripping off your shoulder pips! Whiskey, mob motivation and a higher rank target in range are seldom a good combination for career advancement. You could write a lot of quality material in a self Vindication but one bad potato, and it's all over. Earl was lucky that he could anchor his potato slider to the over consumption of fortified street sherry. It was a tradition at the "cop doo's"—cigars and knock off port. At one time, you lit up a stogie right at the table. Nowadays, the sherry got banged down hard and the cigars civilly torched outside.

It took a long time for Earl to live down the potato caper of 06.' When it came open, the staff wasn't even considered for the super's job. Politically speaking, there was very little appetite for Staff Sergeant Jeans. Earl isn't really that bad. He is just caught up in a greater sense of his own delusional ability. It's a fact, very well known by real cops in the trenches; that most big bosses were full of shit. There was that other time at the adult diaper party that should necessarily be excluded from commentary. After all, these things do happen. One minute you are in diapers and the next minute a staff sergeant—it's really that easy!

Chapter 13
Calling all Cars

Gretchen sat poised over the keyboard and absolutely nothing but bad music danced from her fingertips. She had no desire to call Bliss and inform the big boss that Earl would not be making the "rendez vous." Instead, she would send an email to Bobbi Pichot and hope that it filtered its way up to the lofty heights of Sir Harold. There was a part of her that resented the fact that Earl wouldn't simply call himself. She understood his reasons but it wasn't fair to her. Bliss Landing would, in almost every case, kill the messenger. Of course from Bobbi's point of view it was the Rolicking messenger that would engage the spin cycle. No doubt, once Gretchen called Bobbi she would be obliged to walk into her boss' office and bridge the proverbial gap. District clerks always felt they were a little higher up the pecking order than the Rolicking clerks. Bobbi would likely feel nothing but indignation that another Rolicking crime scene had screwed up her working day. Gretchen resolved herself to her mission at hand and typed;

Hi Bobbi,
Sorry, Earl is tied up at a crime scene in Hill Mountain.
He sends his regrets and cannot make the meeting with
Superintendent Thompson.
Have a great day!
Gretchen

Gretchen knew that Bobbi would not have a great day. Gretchen was also smart enough to know that the, "Have a great day!" thing was really far too catty. Her point of view was that she demonstrated remarkable restraint by not inserting a "happy face." Bobbi would not have the option of simply forwarding the email to Harold. Instead, she would have to enter the inner two window sanctum and personally deliver the dreaded message. Gretchen put on her empathy hat which was, all too often, a very bad fit. She thought to herself how wrong it was for the system to slap back at Earl. After all, it's not as if he planned out the situation in Hill Mountain.

* * * *

P.B. was busy scrambling his efforts. A crime scene that was distanced necessarily meant that he must account for everything. Some of the road gear was already packed. He would also bring Kate's hockey bag of goodies. P.B. looked up at the calendar and laughed to himself, yep—Kate is bang on again! P.B. went into the equipment locker checking portable radios and loading up shotguns. He keyed the portables and made sure that the radios were still encrypted. The encryption would often drop and have to be reloaded. He checked his hockey bag to make sure he had his waterproof suit and hiking boots. ICU always dressed to impress with the very best. Most times you brought your grunge rags along for the ride.

The first act was top hat and tails but the rest of the show was down in the pit. Bad guys didn't have to worry about costumes because their illusion was created within the crime. The caper either worked or it did not. The cops had been lucky because the vast majority of illusions had been laid out poorly. This equated to set, serve and advantage, cops. The trouble was, too many poor illusions and a solid detective becomes complacent.

P.B. liked Kate a lot. She was fair, a good boss and a master of perceiving the sleight of hand. In his day, Earl was solid but now O'Malley dealt more with the "blood and guts" end of the operation. Kate had shown P.B. that a good bad guy, consistent with deception, always laid out a fundamental pattern. The troops had to be able to distinguish between the storyline and a greater sense of truth. Kate could think out the caper. She had the rare gift of street smarts together with a well cultivated sixth sense. In spite of her current monthly cycle of abuse, she was the back bone of the Department.

Brian Connelly, AKA police dog service "Mushy" walked into ICU. Brian was a well preserved outdoorsman who had been a dog man for 16 years. He was one of those old value cops that simply loved what he did best. His dog and partner for "doggie life" was a pure bred German Shepherd by the name of "Licit." No one really knew the history of the dog's name and no one ever asked. Licit was four years old and currently in his prime. He wasn't the best tracking dog that Mushy had ever worked but the dog more than made up for it with personality. Good tracking required that master and dog worked much better than a good marriage. It was up to the master to pick up on the subtle indicators from the dog in order to distinguish between bad guy tracks, sort of evil guy tracks and good guy tracks. Unlike the Sunday night movie, most tracks sucked hard. They were almost always contaminated by normal foot traffic and most times, the offenders wore blue.

Mushy asked, "You ready to roll?"

P.B. replied, "You know the drill. I still have to load up the rest of the gear. Earl can't use his cell in Hill Mountain. By now, he'll likely be pacing and staring off to the north!"

Mushy said, "He'll know we can only move so fast. Is Ident coming up?"

P.B. looking up at Mushy while checking the hockey bag, "Beats me, Harold probably has gotten wind by now ... the Bliss machine is in motion."

Mushy asked, "Did I hear right they found a hand?"

P.B. clarified, "Well, we're not 100% sure on that one Mush, but that's the word right now. I know it sounds like some cheap dime novel or something."

Mushy didn't immediately reply. He looked around ICU at the posters of motorcycles and drug paraphernalia. He always liked to look behind the door. This was the lasting home of Miss Rolicking 1992. In all likelihood, the poster child was a grandma by now!" Kate let the boys keep the picture because by today's standards it was damn tame! It's not like the boys didn't offer to put up some beef cake for their boss, fair is fair. Once things with Kate were, more or less, out of the Rolicking tickle trunk, the boys understood that Miss Rolicking also had a place in Kate's heart.

Behind most police doors lives that "which" cannot be totally exposed. The first thing Earl did when he came into any room was to look immediately behind the door. This was, by his own volition, abnormal behavior. The troops had even seen the boss do this when he went to calls. It was almost as if the absence of a pin-up girl behind a door implied intentional police deception. Mushy commented, "I'm going to gas up the Suburban and head out ... you long behind? Bush is working today maybe we should drag him off?"

P.B. clarified, "I'd love to but the Watch is just too damn short. Grab someone from the Rural side if we can. If not, I guess as the acting "someone" for someone pretty damn important, I'll shake out another body. You can't ride the gravy train without passengers."

P.B stepped out of the ICU and flung his hockey bag over his shoulder.

He walked out through the main office door and into the garage. The slop from Bush's boat still floated above the floor. P.B. thought for a minute that it was a good thing that Earl was trapped out of town. P.B. saw Bush working in the garage and strolled up to him.

In an authoritative voice P.B. suggested, "Earl is stuck in Hill Mountain. You gotta clean up that mess in the garage. Sorry man I can't buy you a ticket for the O.T. ride."

Bush acknowledged his financial fate, "I know you tried no worries. There is lot's going on anyhow. We're backed up with drunks."

P.B. walked out of the office and loaded his bag into the rear of the ICU truck, a 2007 dark blue Explorer. Not bad wheels but hugely beat up from the rural side of operations. Contrary to popular belief, police trucks come with no special suspension. The fleet was all about stock cars and trucks trying to live out super vehicle expectation. This short fall was complemented by vehicles with one headlight, one wiper, flat spare tires, bald tires, broken seat belts, light bars that did light and sirens that did not roar. To add insult to injury, there was also the plethora of "economy minded" vehicles that raised the Department to the "Enviro-North" standard of excellence.

P.B. slammed the rear door. He saw a sticker on the rear bumper which read, "Intensive Crime Unit." He wasn't sure who had put it there. The sticker was originally black on white and now it had been reduced to black on mud. The troops figured that Earl had put it there but P.B. wasn't so sure. He figured Kate had stuck it there just to finger Earl. The sheer art of deception was not limited solely to the world of evil doers.

P.B. made several trips back and forth into the office. He loaded up the computer cases and plastic action chests of detective equipment. The chests had everything from portable printers and USB tokens to extra body armor. He knew there was very little food in Hill Mountain. He'd swing by the sub place and bring some crime scene aperitifs. There was a contingency account in the safe for just such happenings. Sure, you could claim your meals but you wouldn't see an expense check for six weeks or more. P.B. hated the fact that he was often out of pocket more than a grand. There was a meal allowance but most times food cost more outside of Rolicking. In order to submit a claim to Earl you had to submit an actual receipt. Often, there were no formal receipts so P.B. would have the restaurant staff initial candy wrappers, napkins and paper coffee cups. Earl was very supportive of this twisted behavior; the bigger the receipt, the greater the joy. District hated the chore of filing away dirty, bulky coffee cups. P.B. was in the process of walking up to Gretchen's desk when her phone rang. Life stopped dead in the office.

* * * *

Gretchen looked at her call display and stared in disbelief at the District number. It was Harold's phone. She was holding out all hope that Bobbi would call—not Harold himself. Harold could be rude. Especially, if he figured that Earl planted this damn hand just to screw up his day! To drop a severed hand in order to avoid an appointment with a superior would certainly be ill thought out. Earl never did anything he could not skate out of.... Gretchen knew about his sense of slip space. The boss only lived a life of secrets in his own mind. He was totally transparent but the office crew let him relish in his little world. Gretchen did not have voice mail. The call would ring six times then forward automatically to the front desk. If this happened, Gretchen would look like she shuffled off the problem to her colleagues. In reality, she didn't want the problem. On face value, this was somewhat different than intentionally deflecting the attack to some other poor soul.

Bush stumbled into the main office area after hearing the phone while P.B. looked at Gretchen. The old clerk's eyes continued her gaze. It was believed that Gretchen could simply induce "glare halt" at will! She didn't have the face that launched a thousand ships but rather, the beaten face that could sink a small ship. Gretchen's hand reached out to the dirty beige ringing box. She picked up the phone while straightening her back into a more dignified and professional position. "Good morning Rolicking Police!" efficiently greeted Gretchen. There was a quiet pause on the line.

"Superintendent Harold Thompson here, is Staff Sergeant Jeans in?" Gretchen thought to herself, for Christ's sake what the hell is wrong with this guy? He must have seen my email or he must have been told. He must realize that Earl is in Hill Mountain. Maybe he figures that the staff did in fact, cook up this mess.

There was a part of Gretchen that simply wanted to reply, "I'm sorry, he just stepped out for a moment, may I take a message?" In theory, the comment was very true. The leap in logic was admittedly quite generous but nevertheless "out is out." District made a distinction between baby steps and overtime steps. There would be no percentage in evading the truth of the matter. Gretchen often deceived management at the request of Earl. This was very different. If she stretched the truth, it would certainly fly back at her. One other thing, why always those formal titles with District? She didn't try to get everything about police operations, it was a lot like Thanksgiving—one had to accept the bird for what it was.

Gretchen shrugged and replied, "Superintendent Thompson, I am so sorry. Earl is at a crime scene with Detective O'Malley in Hill Mountain. I regret that he cannot be reached by cell."

Harold upped his formal tone, "This is unacceptable I need to speak with him now!"

Gretchen covered the receiver and turned to P.B. and Bush, "I'll pay anyone of you $100.00 to be Earl right now ... okay $200.00."

The collective duo responded as if in perfect harmony, "It's not enough...!" Gretchen hated this part of the job. She never cared about transcribing tapes or filing but she hated being a target for District. She had herself to blame. She should have insisted that Earl leave a number. A number, any number, was the key to redirecting the brass to their rightful target.

Gretchen took a deep breath to calm herself, "Sir, I cannot put Earl on the phone. He is not available. Perhaps, you should try Hill Mountain." The conversation was short lived. Harold hung up the phone. Gretchen was actually quite relieved that the conversation had ended. It was apparent that there was, after all, no such thing as a warm saber.

Chapter 14
Back at the Hill

Kate and Earl remained on the steps of the Co-op store. Their faces reflected more than the usual deep thought. Earl fired out, "What do you think about that damn hand?"

Kate flicked her ash off her smoke and it landed in the tin can. She looked up at the old staff and commented, "It is way too much up front. I just don't get how you can chop off a hand and then what ... I mean why?"

Earl replied, "It strikes me as a creative illusion. Let's face it you almost lost your cinnamon bun over it. The bad guy put it exactly where it would do the most good—or did he...? It wasn't hacked off in the bush or do we know that...? It was chopped off and positioned exquisitely in the cooler. I'm also wondering why not the freezer? Maybe the limb was already frozen and then placed in the cooler to thaw. The actual hack job could have been six months ago! My preliminary guess would be that the cooler represented much better window dressing than the freezer."

Kate said, "The bad guy wouldn't know that we would show up today. Presumably, someone would have gotten into the store or checked up on McIvor by now. They may or may not have seen the hand in the cooler."

Earl elaborated, "And I might add, they may not have even been inclined for whipped cream. We know that the front door was locked. I let you in from the inside. There were no other signs of intrusion. True, I did get in from the back door but there were boxes piled up. I doubt the bad guy left and then figured out a way to get back in and pile the boxes back in place."

Kate smirked at Earl, "Why can't anything with you ever be simple and relatively easy? For instance, here is the body and the bad guy is sleeping upstairs. Just once I'd like it to happen that way."

Earl tossed an eyeball shot below the belt and smiled, "Yeah, but it's not me that carries the omen in her pants! That my dear, is one mean Ouija!"

Kate, "You got that right. Let's knock it around before Harold shows. The money is in the till and a hand in the cooler. The back door is somewhat open, but it could not have been used to exit because of the boxes stacked against it ... right?"

"Detective, you are on the money. But don't forget, we need to know first off who owns the left hand. The best way to do that is to shoot for a fingerprint match and try to find the matching right hand. Who knows, maybe we'll find McIvor and he'll have both his hands. Maybe he was just into the trial marketing of finger food."

"Geez Christ, I'm going to have to listen to these bad liners all day and the rest of the stooges aren't even here yet."

"Actually, the hand notwithstanding, it makes more sense if the front door was unlocked and upon exiting, someone simply secured the door with a key."

"That logic is just so damn Earl. Really ... the bad guy locked the place with a key? In other words, it was all staged for effect? My take is that the hand was left for the shock value. Earl, it's damn sick. Say a customer would have found it. They would have shit bricks!"

Earl smiled and looked down at Kate, "You know something ... you're much smarter than you think. We almost always look at the extreme scenario because our cop minds tell us to. What you just said is, in my elderly opinion, solid shit. That's the reason why you will be much better than I am because you allow yourself the luxury of an emotional response. I was never any good at feelings like you are. This is a huge plus, listen to them and let them jog you in the right direction."

"Staff, you are getting too much like the toga wearing midget at the top of the mountain!" Earl and Kate finished their respective smokes. There was a strange silence for a few minutes. They both enjoyed the back and forth they just exchanged. It was actually much better than bad sex but not as good as swell sex. Once the others arrived, there would be little opportunity for personal reflection. Earl looked to the north. The sounds of the banging dump trucks echoed through the little town. It was now afternoon. A few truckers had filtered off the highway to check out the hula show. Earl thought to himself, that it was a little odd that no one had even come by the store for some milk or ice cream. He shrugged it off. Actually, the Co-op only enjoyed a steady business over the summer. Once the fishermen left, most folks went to Rolicking for the conveniences of life.

* * * *

Mushy and P.B. were just cranking up their trip to Hill Mountain. They had waited their turn at the construction site. No choice, cops going fast or not—everyone must stop for heavy equipment. P.B. thought about the chores at hand once they got there. Visions of command posts, white boards and CCSM danced through his head. He would likely be the "Primary Investigator" on this one. Kate and Earl would want to supervise the more macro scene. Depending on how the day went, he might have to claw back his promotional Vindication and craft up a better story! He had often been told not to call them stories. You never want to trivialize the promotional process. It was, consistent with myth—the brain child of years of superior research. The current promotional process represented the culmination of more than a decade of failed systems. To say the promotion process was less than best would be a huge over statement. Earl always used his own case example to self mock the RCP's obvious shortfalls. The staff talked about how the promotion system is simply a game to be dissected, studied and exploited by the players. P.B. found it hard to argue with that kind of logic.

If the superintendent showed up in Hill Mountain the whole picture could change. When doctrinal managers clashed with working cops anything could happen. As a crime scene, this one is as good as it gets—inside the store, bonus! The down side, it was highly visible and that would be a pain to manage.

P.B. wondered to himself if there would be blood spatter everywhere? He didn't really mind a good crime scene—most of them were fucking mundane. For a change in drama and suspense, it would be nice to reel in a big city file. Most of the junior cops in Rolicking longed for the holy grail of jobs in Bliss. Over the years, there were countless RCP that had bailed from the Department simply because of social hardship. Earl and Kate were the stark exceptions to the rule. The detective couldn't get over the "morbid fact" that they actually liked living in Rolicking.

Typically, a crime scene would be much better managed with a huge exterior perimeter. In this case that would likely be impossible. A two mile perimeter would place the investigational team in the waters of Shallow Lake. They would have to turn over every rock in the little town to get results. Even then, this was far from a smoking gun.

* * * *

Mushy was right behind P.B. in his unmarked "doggie mobile." The dog folks always drove the best—it was that way all over. Even before air conditioning was pretty much standard, the Department paid extra so that the dog would not sweat. Of course, dogs do not sweat but they do get damn hot, sick and die. A dead RCP on the road is one thing, a dead canine asset quite another. Ironically, while the doggie trucks were getting air conditioning, "legend heard tale" that District also paid extra to have the A.M. radios removed from police cars. Even by Earl's standard, that one was a far stretch.

Mushy knew that he had stellar wheels. He lived in the truck and damn it, he expected the best. The team would make up the lost time eaten up from the construction stretch. It was pretty much open road now. Mushy considered himself as much a playful fuck as the next guy. He took pride in being the blunt thorn in Earl's diaper. No one in the RCP had validated the diaper rumors. Hell, incontinence was not something to be joked about. Earl always jabbered on about it but no one knew for sure if he was deflecting the truth. Even if he "pee'd" his pants from time to time, no one would ever blame him.

Mushy looked down. He really didn't have any reason to flip the toggle on the siren but he did it anyway. He knew that Earl would be ear to the wind with Kate. In the spirit of consistent expectation, it would be wrong not to wind up the beast. The old staff always sounded off about the show. Why not raise the curtain and warm up the pit?

Mushy was right, the old staff liked the routine. It underscored the pulse of the investigation.

* * * *

The clash of opposing forces semi-good and totally evil wound the metronome of change. They could not remember the last time there had been a major crime in the wee hamlet. Sure, there were routine beatings, impaired driving and vandalism but certainly nothing that brought about such an auspicious entourage of police vehicles. It was ironic, that in the mindset of Hill Mountain residents, the big city RCP cops had just arrived!

Earl and Kate suspended their respective sentiments while clutching the ash filled tin can. Earl smiled, "The good guys are coming." Earl was glad to see the crew without District trucks in tow. This was the "welcome wagon" offering of friendly folks. This meant that they could line up their collective marbles before the corporate bully came to town. Mushy took his time getting out of the doggie truck. Licit barked nonstop while violently shaking the rear of the truck.

Upon exiting, Mushy banged his fist on the truck and hollered, "Settle the fuck down!" Leaping off the floor boards, P.B projected himself out of the Explorer. Earl looked at him and tilted his head to the right, as if to say, "Kindly fuck off." The old staff was somewhat surprised that he didn't have the CCSM computer and overtime form in hand!

Earl spoke first while gesturing to Mom's, "Let's see if we can't step off the front steps a little. I'll fill youz in."

The group shuffled off into the driveway area between Mom's and the Co-op. Earl huddled the small group in a tight scrum and bent his waist at a 30 degree angle. He waived his fingers for the rest of the group to do the same. Earl wrapped his arms around Kate's and P.B.'s shoulders. Mushy folded his arms outside the circle and looked on with a snide and bemusing look. Kate also gave Earl an inverted smirk as if to suggest that "decoding" was not an option. For the most part, the troops enjoyed the "visual cool aid" as refreshingly served up by the staff.

Earl leaned into the circle and uttered, "We have a hand in a cooler and some blood out back. The blood could be the dogs. The dog is a nice dog, no worries there. Now, get out there and figure this one out."

Mushy was the first one to laugh out loud. He blurted out, "Fuck, I'm sure glad this is not 3:00 A.M. in the morning 'cause I, sure as shit, would not be here."

It was Kate's role to set up some sort of selective strategy. In reality, the Ident folks should be first up. They needed to do their thing in the store. Ident, like ambulances, should arrive first but almost never did. Earl had already trampled all over the store but such was life, no choice initially—you had to walk over a crime scene to get to the peanuts.

The police dog continued to bark. Mushy said, "I'm going to let the devil out for a piss."

P.B. asked Kate, "Where do you want me to start?"

Kate and Earl replied as a chorus, "At the beginning." This line had been a standard for years. It was used to audibly rein in the younger cops. It was critical that a supervisor double clutch and slow down the Validation spins. The idea behind the comment is to anticipate a problem and then stop, drop and roll before the fire hits. Most investigations run into snags not so much because of a failure to react but because of well motivated haste.

Until Ident got there the crew would focus on trying to find McIvor. It was logical. The owner of the store was tied naturally into the investigation because of the original robbery. He still hadn't showed which was awkwardly weird in itself. There was this hand thing and the store hadn't opened as expected. It was most odd for a town that was normally anchored to routine.

Kate looked at P.B., "Right now let's just buy some time. I need you to canvass the north side of the street. Let's keep folks thinking we are looking into the prior robbery. Right now, we just want to try and locate McIvor."

Earl looked approvingly at Kate, "Good call on that one. The less things get stirred up the better." P.B. grabbed his Rolicking issued voice recorder and went off across the street. Someone had to stay by the store and keep folks out. Fundamental to low keyed security, was its implementation with the least amount of speculation. Earl sauntered over to the Crown Vic and pulled out his midnight black 600 dernier nylon encrusted brief case. He walked over to the store window, unzipped the case and located a rectangular chunk of metal. He placed the contents on the wall of the building. The sign read simply, "Closed by Order of The Health Department." Earl didn't remember where he got the sign. Maybe, he stole it from Jenn? The sign had come in handy at numerous crime scenes.

Earl stepped back. The marquee looked damn good complete with a knock off provincial logo and French translation. Earl surmised that the locals would have no problem believing that the piss smell was somehow tied into a macro health issue. The old staff had several other signs. They included "Handicap," "Police Officer on Duty," "Insecticides in Use," "Caution Methane Gas," "Closed - Rail Derailment" and of course, "Closed by Order of the Liquor Commission." The later was particularly effective when the cops just wanted to slow down business into a bar. By the time the owner realized the sign was up, he just assumed that he was having an unusually slow night. Earl looked at the crew and they looked back at him—there was non-verbal consensus.

Chapter 15
The Past

Melanie Jeans and Ashley Funk found themselves in "Raven's Roast." Raven's was your quintessential trendy, friendly and terribly convenient coffee shop. Ashley was still in her flag girl fluorescent striped orange overalls. She was noticeably self conscious by her lack of fashion detailing. There was really no need to care as the shop was filled with contractors, well dressed people and most everything in between. The key to the washroom was found by the cash. It was fastened securely by a foot long chunk of hockey stick. The shop was painted drab brown but was laden with extras that were more befitting a candy than a coffee shop.

There was the ice cream freezer complete with a hardy assortment of three kinds of ice cream. It was an old time freezer with the obligatory "see through" and slide up chest door. Frozen yogurt was typically on short supply. There wasn't much demand in Rolicking. On display was an assortment of double iced and candy sprinkled donuts. Dainties did not exist in the North. The essence of a "mille-feuille" was presumed by most to be an incorrigible position in the bedroom. The food was either fresh or "week old dead." Everything else was deemed middle of the road available. The old paper "tip cup" with folded in paper handles enticingly rested on the counter. There were several cross outs of server names and one could only speculate, that the current name "Debbie" was actually the lady behind the counter.

The girls had grown up together. Their formative years consisted of childhood sleepovers accompanied with all the spit rituals associated with secret clubs. At the beginning, it was the "Royal Order of Pixies," then later, the various organized teenage clubs. Ashley had decided to keep her summer job until the construction gig was over in November. She expected her dad to gripe. Instead, he supported her on the principle of both working hard and taking some extra time. In fact, after the murder, he felt it best that she wait awhile to go back to school.

Sergeant Funk had made special arrangements to home school her himself. If Ashley was to be schooled at home, there was really no choice. Ashley's Mom had left them almost a year ago. Her mom was a city girl at heart. The North was never her preferred lifestyle. Her dad had tried to make her mom live his life. Over time the plan failed miserably. Ashley's mom never had a regular job in Rolicking. Her accumulated free time often equated to hyperactive bitching time.

Mike Funk had tried to cope with the situation but he kept digging himself in deeper. Rolicking provided everything that a "low maintenance" consumer could ever want. In reality, whether it be a large center or a small city, shopping is typically vested in the "dot com" cyber store of choice. The lingering rub ... some folks were never happy, unless they were physically engaged in the turmoil of the big city. For some, the pursuit of luxury often exceeds a greater sense of satisfaction derived from the known.

Once "Mushroom Pizza" (MP) opened it was the one and only place to go. It represented neither cuisine nor dive. It was a known for its simple yet predictable draft beer like consistency. Folks in Rolicking loved culinary stability. Mike always felt that people in the city always looked too damn rushed to be that happy. The sergeant could have been happier. Unfortunately he skated right, when Earl stick handled left. Mike always secretly hoped that Ashley would finally end up on Earl's side of the rink.

Melanie asked, "How was your day?"

Ashley replied, "Dusty as hell, it hasn't rained for weeks. You can't really win. It's either the bugs or the wind. The bugs are the worse. They get in your hair."

Melanie said, "Yeah, I was lucky teaching piano all summer and babysitting. I don't have the tan you have but way less bites. How much time do you have?"

Ashley looked at her cell and responded, "Almost 4:00 P.M. I have to beat it for supper soon. No major rush, I'll text my Dad. He worries a lot ever since the murder. As long as I say I'm with you and not some dreaded boy, no worries. He has self captured himself again, working on another car. I don't know what he'd do without the renos. It's nice that the phone has stopped ringing but he still gets up early for those 5:00 A.M. workouts."

Melanie asked, "What kind of car is he fixing now?"

Ashley replied, "It's one of those old Mazda sports cars. It is a real nice red color … that's the best part. He is putting in an awesome sound system. He might let me take it for spin after it's done. He gets real clingy once he fixes them up. Dad is always worried about scratches and dents."

Melanie took a tempered sip of coffee. She held the big white and green cup up with two hands. Her gaze at her girlfriend was stream lined over the rim of the cup. Both girls were about the same stature. It was more habit than an actual need to peer over the cup. Although they had grown up together, there were some things they kept to themselves. Girlfriends almost always give up little secrets—the big ones are much more deeply cached. The girls had their share of secrets. Melanie was more "bubbly" than her counterpart and more apt to open up. Ashley had a very uneasy streak about her. It wasn't so much that she relished the fast lane—it was more the case that the fast lane rode her.

The girls knew that there was plenty happening in Rolicking. For the most part, there was so much that could not be shared with parents. It was lame to suggest that parents didn't get it. The fact of the matter is they could not be expected to "get" what they cannot know. Cop parents are just like doctors and dentists. They always look after other people first. All the kids knew about the gangs and dope. They were everywhere—all around the school. Parents, consistent with our expectation, always rambled on about drugs. Their rant was usually sparked after the immediate viewing of a public service announcement or a youthful arrest. Most parents worked long hours. There wasn't the built in time to digest street speculation.

Melanie put down the cup and hunched over the small, beaten up round table. To a certain extent, the girls were physically contained by the voluminous plastic flowers and plants that encircled the table. Melanie absorbed Ashley all suited up in her orange and florescent overalls. The construction gig helped her get by the issues. She was making lots of money and would return to school in the next couple of weeks. In a sense, it was good all round' that her dad had made arrangements with the principal. It wasn't like the sergeant to take such a keen interest in self schooling. Melanie thought to herself that her dad would never have lasted one hour with an Elizabethan poetry book!

Melanie coddled her spoon and spun it around her coffee a couple of times. She watched the ripples mellow out and then bang into the rim. Ashley picked up on the subtle awkwardness of the moment. Like all good friends, the girls retained an enviable comfort within lingering silence. Today, there was much more pressure in the air.

The only difference between their respective beverages was the dollop of whipped cream that floated triumphantly on the surface of Melanie's cup. Melanie had learned a long time ago that the very presence of a garnish in an otherwise "normal" coffee would drive her dad nuts. The fact of the matter was that she didn't even like the topping that much. It was just habit now and sort of a running joke in the family. In all fairness, whipped cream and sprinkles notwithstanding, she got along great with her dad. No choice now, the ladies at Raven's had learned quickly to just "auto fling" the big dollop. In Rolicking you took what you were given—resistance was short lived.

Melanie commented, "It will be great when you come back to school … I miss you around."

Ashley looked down at the table and took a moment to think, "It won't be easy the first little while. I've thought about it a lot but sooner or later, I have to take the plunge … right? The trouble with flagging is that you often have too much damn time to think."

Melanie solidly reassuring, "I'll be there—no worries. If you feel uneasy, I totally understand. You've been through a lot. I know your dad is with you on this one."

Ashley clarified, "My mom called from the city last night. They got into it. My dad never told her that he was suspended from work—I didn't either. How can she hate us so much as to leave Rolicking? I'll never forgive her. One thing for sure … Dad has his moments but its way better not listening to all the yelling. Parents don't get how bad they sound. I used to just walk away and go to my room. You remember the fights. You were over sometimes—I was always so embarrassed."

Melanie leaned over and tossed out her napkin. She pulled at the napkin holder to get a clean one out. The napkin container was stuffed full. Melanie yanked and ended up with more paper than napkin. She thought to herself that she really didn't want to go down old ground with Ashley. She also knew that her friend had no one else to talk with. Melanie had learned to keep up the phony smile and nod politely. She would dig a little deeper once the timing was right.

Melanie asked, "What are you doing tonight?"

Ashley replied, "I'm just hanging. My back is killing me from all that standing on the road. I have a lawn chair but I'm always up and down … you can't really use it. It's more of a stuff holder than a bum holder."

Melanie thought for a moment, "Guess, I had it too easy. My dad said it was okay if I didn't work. He wanted me to hang with him lots at the cabin—he misses the old days. He won't let me get rid of my old dollhouse. I'm glad I got the babysitting job, at least there's that…"

Ashley offered, "Enjoy it girl while you can! We'll both be heading down south for school and work. It will be nice when we'll be off on our own. If my mom thinks I'm going to go and see her in Winnipeg, she has another thing coming. Dad hates the crowds, says it's too dangerous."

Melanie replied, "I know exactly what you mean. I have no worries at my end—my dad is totally bushed. He'll never leave Rolicking. He says he can't wait to retire but he'd better damn well find something to do! He'll drive me nuts if he is just kicking around the house." Sensing timing, Melanie put down the coffee cup, while looking down and away asked, "Do you miss him...?" Melanie knew that she should not have asked her friend like that. It was just sort of tacked on, it happened because it must. The comment couldn't be taken back, some never can.

The silence was no longer comfortable. Ashley just stared and said nothing while Melanie reached for her hand. At the same time and in direct eye sight, Melanie looked in the corner and noticed a poster of a cartoon kid holding an enormous ice cream cone. It was the kind of graphic ad that whimsically screamed out to be ignored. The sign lifted her emotional load for a brief second. Melanie's eyes refocused back on her friend.

"What do you mean?" Ashley replied, while shrugging her shoulders.

Melanie clarified, "I mean 8 Ball."

Ashley really knew what Melanie inferred but it simply wasn't to be talked about. Well sometimes with those crisis councilors—they hounded all the time. Ashley thought how sick she was of the so called support mechanisms that adults dumped on kids.

Ashley said, "I miss him all the time. I knew that he wasn't the kind of guy that a girl would marry. Hell, I couldn't even bring him around the house. It drove Dad insane. It was good of you to cover for us. I should have gone to the big funeral in Winnipeg. He wouldn't hear of it. It was like the relationship didn't exist. It's not like I was doing dope. He did his thing ... I knew about it but it wasn't tossed in my face. Sometimes, this cop kid thing, you know ... sucks! Maybe it's just as well I didn't go to Winnipeg. There could have been other chicks."

Melanie felt awkward and started to rise. She asked, "You want a refill?" Ashley passed her hand over the top of her cup indicated she had enough. Both of the girls got up from the table. It was self serve all around which included the clean up. The plastic plants vibrated when they got up. It was impossible not to brush against the big leaves.

* * * *

Strange thing about these plants, they almost look like they could have been listening. If they could have listened, they would have known the whole story all along. 8 Ball and Ashley came to Raven's regularly for coffee. Sometimes the cops were also there. As long as her dad didn't show there was never a problem. Like any small town, chances were that the attending cops would gladly spin out the sordid details to their sergeant. Ashley hated the way that cops treated cops. It was as if they truly enjoyed taking turns slapping each other down. Like Melanie, Ashley had grown up with the phone ringing in the night. It wasn't normal that it rang so much. Mike didn't always go to the office but he always answered the phone. It had gotten much worse when cell phones came to Rolicking. You can't very well hide from them. Her dad used to sleep in the basement so that the ringing wouldn't wake up the whole house. The little girl never liked the fact that her dad was two floors away. Life should have been much simpler.

Chapter 16
The Product

Sergeant Mike Funk sat in his garage hovering over his '86 Mazda RX-7. It felt right for him to be elbow deep in thick black grease. The stress of not working was driving him mental. Ever since the incident at the office, he was "more or less" reined into his home turf. There were also some minor diversions like fishing at Shallow Lake.

The garage was barely big enough to contain one vehicle. The house was circa 1965. It was dressed in white clapboard peeling siding. The front door was prefaced with the Rolicking issued sideways front steps. The frost heaves knocked around a house pretty good. Brick isn't that prevalent in the North. Good thing because it would surely crack. The sergeant had tried to keep up the house. Instead, routine maintenance always defaulted to calamity driven priority.

Mike considered himself somewhat lucky. He had a heated garage with a small shop. The shop did not lack any type of tool. There was literally a sea of black and yellow everywhere. The smell of fuel stabilizer and automotive lacquer clung to the air. Mike had his air compressor, sockets, key duplicator, voltage meters, paint sprayers, metal cutters and even old arc welder. He wouldn't make it on an "auto challenge show" but conversely, he wouldn't star on an episode of "right out losers." He'd been playing with and restoring vehicles since he was a kid.

The RX-7 looked totally out of place in Rolicking. The sergeant knew that it would fit nicely into a big city future. It was candy apple red blanketed with a midnight black interior. The seats were a little beat up from prior abuse. They would have to be replaced. With a little work, the rest of the interior could be salvaged. Mike knew he could make things work. There was little choice.

Ashley often helped him with the cars. His little girl had grown into an attractive teenager. The time had come where she gave Mike major worry. There was always gang talk in Rolicking. It's not that you could see the bangers on every corner but they were obviously there. Adults could actually live here and never really be sure if the gangs were out. The kids always knew. There was every opportunity to make some major coin with really very little effort. Mike thought he understood the parameters of the game. It was there to be played. Understandably, his family was not a part of the equation. Mike preferred defined business arrangements. He detested the sinking feeling associated with the alternative. The Department had made him feel out of control but in reality, the sergeant knew it was his fault. It wasn't intentional—it had spun out that way. He had no idea why he winged the stapler at P.B. It just sort of happened. Who ever expected a gay guy to break it to his boss that he needed paternity leave? Is the Department expected to flex for each and every twisted social convention?

Mike walked over to the work bench and changed the satellite radio to extreme 70's rock. He was going on 44 now and rap was out of the question. He had served with the Department for almost the same amount of time as Earl. The good sergeant always admired the staff. However, at the core level they were very different people. It hadn't started out that way twenty years ago but life changed all that....

It's funny how two sensible guys can both go down the same path. There evolves a juncture but for no apparent reason one goes left and one goes right. Once they arrive at the same destination they can't help but be different people. Earl had his core group of friends and enemies. Friends and enemies almost always circle around decision makers. If you were the kind of person that never made a decision, chances are you wouldn't be especially hated or liked. Oddly, the old sergeant felt he rested somewhere in between. Just once, he'd like a little respect and recognition. In spite of Earl's loud mouth, reverence from the crew came about so genuinely.

Mike exited the side door of the garage and shuffled off to a small shed at the back of the lot. He always made sure that all the doors were shut behind him. He carried an old duck colored electrician's tool bag with hooped black handles. It was a faded and looked more like it belonged in a dirty trunk than clutched in the mechanic's hands. Mike unlocked the door and walked into the old wood shed. There was the expected assortment of motor oil containers, old lamps, snow shovels, hockey sticks and a green wheel barrow. There was also the big red snow blower which sat waiting for the winter oil change. Sitting on the top shelf was an old microwave oven. Presumably; awaiting finality at the dump, he had put it there years ago. It was a first generation microwave whose very existence, suspended both time and evolution. It's big silver handle and bakelite knobs left the impression that the appliance would better suited in an old radio shop. Mike reached out and opened the oven door. He removed a duct taped wrapped green garbage bag. The sergeant unzipped the tool bag and simultaneously took out another opaque plastic bag that was also duct taped. The door to the microwave was smoke black. It either came that way from the manufacturer or something previously exploded remained lacquered to the small window. Mike looked down and made sure the green garbage bag and contents were completely zipped in the tool bag. He put the other plastic wrapped package into the microwave and closed the door. Like the door rattling from another cop era, he pulled the handle on the shed—it was locked.

While Mike walked back to the garage he stopped and played briefly with his husky dog, "Andi." Mike couldn't remember how the mutt got that handle but it had firmly stuck. The dog pulled playfully while tugging on the tool bag. Andi obviously enjoyed Mike's company. The sergeant looked up and noticed that dark storm clouds were now making their way into Rolicking. No way to tell, it would either be a good boomer or blow over. When the wind blew from the west, things were sure to change. It really didn't matter either way, there was good protection in the garage.

The sergeant thought about the office suspension. It would likely blow over in time. He had seen other guys go through the same thing. You just had to weather out the nasty ride. He looked up at the garage door motor, totally screwed. It had to be replaced before winter. It was a big door and lifting it manually would be difficult in the cold. Ashley would never cope. The October jobs for any guy's time line were much bigger than any other time of the year. This year was different. He had too much damn time. Andi barked loudly in the backyard obviously objecting to the end of play. He was now 14 years old but acted more like a puppy each day. Mike shrugged off the thought. In time, no doubt, Andi the wonder dog will set the record for the longest living mutt in captivity!

The sergeant went into the shop area of the garage and closed the inner door. He unzipped the canvas bag and sliced the duct tape carefully with a box cutter. He looked at the hundreds of bills in the bag. He could only think of what this money would mean to Ashley. There was supposed to be $75,000 in 50's.

He had to give final positioning some good thought. The hatchback design of the car provided more than enough room in the quarter panels. On more than one occasion, he had simply put the money inside the driver's seat stuffing. The cops were getting smarter. There might be trace product on the money but generally speaking, money wasn't a huge issue with dogs. Once the bucks left Rolicking the money would be cleaned off in Winnipeg. It was nothing to move $75,000. This could easily be done at the Casino or through any bar. He was glad that he didn't have to worry about the Winnipeg end—that was the risky part of business. Up here in Rolicking he had established his comfort zone. If there was ever a Rolicking City version of the "import and export" business—Mike Funk owned it.

The good news was that the restoration business was booming! Mike was more than square with the tax folks on that one. He paid his tax installments as he must. A legitimate business could even deduct the price of garbage bags and duct tape. Everything that was reworked or customized was always meticulously detailed. The tax people loved records so why should he disappoint? A copy of the before and after shot went down the road with the vehicle—clients ate this stuff up.

Let's face it, were the police likely to cut open a newly restored leather seat? It's not like it couldn't happen but it was very unlikely to occur without significant probable cause. The photo journal represented both a support prop for the runner and lasting proof for the buyer. Mike had learned a long time ago that cover enhancements were the absolute key to success. Cops and tax men were no different than anyone else. If the story was credible, convincing and supported with documentary evidence then it played out real. The margin for error between a convincing role and a discovered rip was almost nil. Good cops need to create margin while bad guys have it built into production.

He didn't consider himself to be a bad guy. He was both the creator and entrepreneur of a lucrative part time job. He did it not for himself but for his family. The money allowed him to buy salvaged cars, fix them up and make an honest profit. After all, he had a Rolicking City business license which necessarily meant he was legit.

Mike looked at the rear of the car. He took a few more pics for a possible next time job. There was the photo journal that went down the road and there was also Mike's business journal. If there was one thing he had learned in policing, it was to document the hell out of everything. Mike laid the driver's seat on its side and took photos of the bottom. He removed a piece of nylon material that covered up the foam padding. There wasn't enough room under the seat. With a lot of vehicles it's not an absolute. You have to look all over a car before you could find just the right place. The best storage areas of any vehicle will not show up in a workshop manual.

The old New Yorker's were the best. They had tons of room all over to conceal just about anything. Like a painter admiring his work, Mike strolled around the car contemplating his options. He opened the hatch and then the lower compartment which housed the otherwise useless, spare tire. Mike shook his head when he looked at the "wagon like" flimsy tire. He'd have to throw in a real spare just in case. No one hid anything in a tire these days. In fact, most guys went out of their way to leave the spare exactly as expected.

Under the tire there was a carpeted area and then structural steel. He could consider cutting out a metal opening but that would scar up the surface. It had to stay stock as all hell. If he chose to scar up the body he had to introduce the impression of purpose. Because of the hatchback design there was room in the rear quarter panels for flush mounted speakers. It would mean some minor rewiring but any positive change would only serve to beef up the old journal. The cops would certainly pull the speaker baffles and some hot shot rookie would fire up the stereo. Everything would work just fine. Mike removed the left and right quarter panel exterior plastic panels. Those bloody plastic clips almost always broke. Not a problem, the mechanic had a collection of vintage fasteners.

He strolled into his shop and sorted through some electrical materials. He came out with two matching six inch speakers and baffles. He cut an opening in the plastic. Behind the speakers were natural cavities in the metal. He would have to repackage the money into tubular containers that could bend along the wheel well. He had several sock like nylon beer coolers that were about six inches in diameter and four feet long. They really weren't much for cooling beer but they worked just fine for product and currency. The coolers had a weird sling arrangement much like an arrow quiver—perfect. The rest of the rigging would seem most natural.

Mike went back into the shop area again. He cut open the money pack and removed the bills. The sergeant was clearly sweating. He thought to himself how much he hated this moment. Earl always talked about slip space. The risk was all his now. He had tried to dream up a backup plan. How would he skate out of a compromised situation? "Geez Dear ... I was just putting away some coin for a rainy day!" or better still, "Hi Ashley, glad you found me I was just going to peel off some 50's for tuition." Cash almost always comes dark, dirty and liquid. You can pour it anywhere, anytime. It could be moved anywhere in the prairies especially the 50's. There was a time when storekeepers would look at a 50 dollar bill like it was big money. Today's 50's were now the ten spots of the 60's. Mike stared down at a bill and he chuckled for a brief moment at the "Musical Ride" graphic on the paper—somewhat ironic in the big picture.

The money fit in the two tubular containers with ease. Mike looked at the clock it was now 4:15 P.M. There was just one hour before Ashley came home.

The mechanic took a 24 inch length of black 16 gauge automotive wire and attached one end to each of the cooler slings. On the other ends, he crimped an open end wire connector with a heat shrinkable yellow insulating sleeve. After crimping, he then inserted the coolers through the metal holes and down into the right and left quarter panel cavity areas. The 50's slid down nice and tight. The containers rode low with the added weight of the money. They could easily be pushed farther down in the cavity and out of sight. The cargo wouldn't even rattle on the trip down. He held onto the newly crimped ends of wire and fastened them to the supposed grounding screws. The end of the "fish wires" could be seen but they looked exactly like every other grounding wire. Once the product was in Winnipeg it would be easy to reel up.

Mike once again, meticulously inspected the other ground wires and screws to make sure that the additional hardware looked exactly like stock. Like a cabinet maker antiquing a fine table, Mike aged the insulators with a heat gun and melted the plastic just a touch. The illusion was never complete until everything looked "together." He took out a jar of trailer bearing grease and rubbed it lightly on the surface of the screws.

The presentation equaled that of a fine French restaurant. Even if a cop searched and pulled the speakers, there would be no reason to look further. Only if you were in the inside end of the business would you know where to find the product. Mike always put a great deal of thought into the effect. If there is one thing he had learned from real bad guys was, how not to get caught. It was odd that so much work was being put into a project that in all likelihood would not be seen.

Mike the mechanic continued to work at the rear panels and installed the speakers and baffles. The worse was over. He could take his time now with the retro fit, his mind wandered …. The office suspension had definitely slowed things down. 8 Ball's mistake had cost everyone both time and money. The sergeant had no use for street hoods. They existed for no one's good. The bangers were the real crack whores in society. The sergeant despised the fact that any of them would even look at Ashley. Ashley knew how he felt. He should have kept a closer eye out—like Earl did with Melanie. Of course, Earl also had Judy. What was done was done. The sergeant had learned never to look back. Fate is to be greeted for what it becomes.

Once finished, the car would be driven to Winnipeg. Typically, Mike threw the keys at one of the young coppers who just wanted a quick break in the city. They would drive the car down and he would fly them back to Rolicking. It was all a legitimate business expense to the tax man. Even if Bush was out on the highway checking for dope runs, the young coppers would just crank up the tunes and wave. The mechanic couldn't help but laugh to himself. He pondered the visual imagery of 50 dollar bills bouncing down the road—the proud horsemen lances drawn.

The money side of things was totally backstopped. Mike didn't have absolute control of the rest of the business. This always posed him a great deal of concern. You can't maintain absolute control unless you do all the work yourself. You could be the very best businessman and still end up in a spreadsheet on some distant hard drive. Once you give up some control then you necessarily expose yourself to further interest. This is exactly what happened in the office. He had to make sure there was never going to be another stapler.

Chapter 17
Here Comes Management

Earl watched P.B. bang on doors on the north side of the street. It was now late in the afternoon. His appointment with Superintendent Thompson was blown beyond belief. Earl wondered to himself if the boss would call or what? Once the scientists got there he would be obligated to call in a status report to Harold. Typically, this type of call would generate more questions than answers. Management always wanted to be in the loop. Earl and Kate knew the drill. It was just, more times than not, the loop was never complete at the beginning. The truth of the matter was that the loop was really a flat line at the start of any major file.

The story was compelled, by virtue of need, to unfold without tangible links. Earl thought to himself about some plausible first lines to the boss, "Geez Sir, we haven't found the rest of the body yet, keep you posted." No, that wouldn't do at all. In a perfect world, his first call would have to provide greater detail. To call a superior looking like you did sweet fuck all, offered up zero percentage. There was also that issue of the warrant to get back in the Co-op. Of course, it would read poorly without some redeeming detail from a third party source. There was essentially, at this point, the noticeable absence of a time line. Most warrants need something more substantial then a limb of ground chuck in a cooler.

Earl turned his attention to Kate, "Hey, I'm just thinking about the warrant. Did I miss something or do we only have squat? More or less a chunk of meat missing an expiry date?"

Kate looked up at her boss, "Right now we have a fucking hand, no storyline and certainly no time frame anchoring said hand to foul play. I hope that P.B. can beef things up a little!"

Earl shook the dust off his suit coat while jiggling some coins in his pants pockets. He commented, "Now it's your turn for the bad jokes." The sun was now fading over the otherwise somber main street. The banging of the dump trucks had stopped about an hour earlier. The tranquility of the duo's voices seemed much more resonant then they had been all day.

The staff pondered the ongoing situation while knocking around his current risk analysis. Even if P.B. rolled over a rock and there was a mouse turd, it would still be added detail. Earl conjured the possibilities out loud, "Yes Sir, we have discovered a mouse turd under a rock. Unfortunately, we have no fucking idea how said mouse rolled the rock back upon the turd." Earl was at the point in life where a simple turd would always harbor a greater mystery. A smarter cop would have ended discussion and rolled the rock back on the turd. There was a part of the staff that severely detested administrative games. Conversely, he also knew that there was that other, much darker side of his psyche, that thrived on organizational play. Much like the game of life and death someone in management always drew the shorter straw. Even if the investigation played out perfectly, complete with bad guy in cuffs; there would always be financial posturing and finger pointing. Earl thought it was always odd that those with the cleanest fingers—always did most of the pointing.

The background silence became unbearable, "When do you think Ident will get here?" It was one of those contrived questions that was so uncharacteristic of Kate.

Earl looked down, butted out his smoke and replied, "If I was them, I would have been here an hour ago. In another hour we will lose daylight. This will truly suck as we'll have to try and hold the scene overnight. I might have to consider bringing in some provincial trucks to back up the Health Department sign. Inspector Jenn ... what's her name? You know, with the Health Department ... what the hell's her last name?" Kate shrugged obviously not able to reply.

Earl felt obligated to fill in the absence of natter with his own innate reflection, "Well maybe worse case, Health can go in the store under the Health Act and seize the hand. Either way, the hand has to go. It's not like we can just open the store up and advertise body parts on special!"

Kate replied, "Earl, enjoy the smoke 'cause it's going to eventually clear big time when Mr. Pip's shows up."

Earl chuckled under his breath and asked, "You think he's coming here?"

Kate looked straight at Earl. It was not the look of being in shit but simply, the detective's turn to play the company's advocate. She commented, "I know you don't have much regard for him but you really left him no choice. He can't just sit in Bliss and fume because you blew the appointment. He can't even call you. Well, he could but … I can't see him trying to reach you through Mom's. He is going to have to mount up and get his ass in here."

Earl looked down at his partner. For a strange second he found himself in the odd position of being short for words. He simply replied in an uncustomary monotone voice, "Makes sense." There were times when the old staff liked to mix up words. There were other times, especially with Kate—where she said it best for both of them.

Earl looked off to the southwest. Mushy was still playing with his dog in back of Mom's. He had the dog off leash but far enough from McIvor's dog. Mushy chucked a rubber toy after spinning it with the attached bright yellow rope. Earl watched the toy sail through the air. The straightened rope followed like a tail. The rubber toy bounced several times on the ground. Licit instantly leaped on his make shift rubber victim. Like a hooker in the throes of a big pay day, the big shepherd shook his head violently on the hard rubber.

* * * *

Kate turned north towards P.B.'s movements on the opposite side of the street. They way he flitted from door to door didn't leave the impression that he was getting much mileage. Kate grabbed the portable radio that P.B. had transported. She held up the radio and keyed the transmit button, "P.B, Kate, P.B." There was no reply from the junior detective. Kate wasn't surprised he was probably tied up with a witness. While she pondered the situation she saw an old man stagger across the far end of town by the garage. He had those classical unsure and wobbly legs so customary in the North. She watched him drift out of sight then down and under the small bridge. Almost every little town had one of these old men. Kate had seen one just about everywhere.

Kate thought briefly to herself about all the clothes that hadn't been bought in Bliss. Crime scenes always turned up at the most inconvenient of times. She thought to herself about the left hand. She was damn mad at herself. She should have taken a closer look at it while they were in the store. There was really no way to do that without disturbing the garlic dip and nudging those cheese slices. A detective might get away with the soft poke of a chip dip. However, the rule book could not excuse the prod of a cheesy oil product.

She fired her attention back to Earl which, in turn, placed her directly in the same line as Mushy and Licit. The duo watched the game of fetch for several minutes. Mushy could have passed as a big league chucker by the way he flung the toy high in the air. The dog didn't seem to have a real good sense of depth. Licit intently followed the toy's descent. He would target it, as if perfectly orchestrated; only to take it off the nose. The hit didn't seem to matter that much to the dog. Kate watched for awhile. It was almost as if the dog understood that the necessary pain of getting hit served a greater purpose. There was garbage and obstacles all over the back lot but Licit seemed to enjoy the challenge of the hunt. Cop dogs were high energy by their very nature. The dog knew that he was in Hill Mountain for a reason. Dogs had no inbred desire to wait for scientists or warrants. It was Mushy's job to keep the dog keenly aware should they be deployed yet, rested enough for the long haul.

At that very moment, Earl and Kate were jogged by a black Impala and a dark blue Suburban that swung into town. The vehicles brought about that instant impression reminiscent of two drivers looking for a lost funeral procession. As if absorbed in the pageantry of the event, the deliberate vehicles rolled painfully down the main drag. With no whistle sounding, the convoy eventually ground to an abrupt halt.

Earl looked at Kate, "Well at least we know that Ident is here. That is a good thing."

The black Impala was one of the raided vehicles that were taken out of the operational fleet. The black one was Harold's. It was very well known in the North. The Suburban held the Ident crew aptly described as, "The Keeper's of Science, Fact and Sleight of Hand." They were capable of razzling and dazzling accompanied with a chorus of chemicals and concoctions. Perhaps, it was their show that Earl so cherished. For some reason, the old staff had tons of patience for Ident. The scientists would first attack the outdoor scene. Hopefully, they would surface something of value for the warrant. The RCP referred to the warrant author as the paper writer. If someone had been "P.W.'ed" in Rolicking City—it was not necessarily a bad thing! Kate butted out her smoke in the tin can and tossed it out of sight. She took out a piece of gum and offered one to her partner.

* * * *

Earl grabbed at the foil wrapping and excised a stick of gum. The old staff couldn't help but notice that there was a hanging feeling in the air. It was much like static electricity before a storm or the wife's look after that third cup. Women around the world would always deny the existence of the third cup stare but "guyhood" confirmed its very existence. All males know that a couple of drinks were fine but there was something innate about the third cup to the fairer sex. For a fleeting moment, Earl wondered if Coral had ever given Kate the third drink stare.

The situation was now very fragile—much more so than a crime scene. Bad guys were easy; it was the good guys' bosses that needed to be delicately managed. If Earl could text the boss worth shit this would have been the perfect time. *Duh Earl*, the cell phones don't work! Sometimes those kids didn't have such poorly contrived notions. *Note to self*, personal interaction wasn't all it was cropped up to be.

Superintendent Harold Thompson exited the passenger side of the Impala. His driver and current Executive Officer, Sergeant Bernie exited the driver's seat. Sergeant Bernie had been Harold's driver for years. Of course, he had other administrative responsibilities. However, on the major roadies Harold always had Bernie drive. Bernie had a surname but everyone around called him Sergeant Bernie—it stuck, so why fuck with consistency? He even had a name tag over his pocket which confirmed his identity as one, "Sergeant Bernie." In reality, the good sergeant had a last name—Pzielbriefzki (with a silent "b"). Logically, Sergeant Bernie hung like glue. In a sense, the absence of formal protocol was inconsistent with the teachings of Bliss Landing. Earl surmised to himself that Sergeant Bernie's name tag was probably a chapter from the good Dr. Shelby. You know … the part about getting back to basics and being more approachable. Too bad Harold hadn't drawn the same inference.

Earl and Kate looked on. There were simply no words that could describe the majesty of the moment. Earl could have simply walked over to his boss instead he stood motionless. Kate started to move and Earl, like a crossing guard, fired out his right hand to stop her. It wasn't done with the objective of tact or diplomacy. Earl commented under his breath, "Steady up Detective!"

After exiting his vehicle, the boss moved very abruptly and walked immediately up to Earl. Like Earl, the District boss was over six feet tall. However, Harold was noticeably a lot thinner in stature. The superintendent wore his forge cap peaked with regulation gold braid that truly dignified the part. The big bosses in District always had lots of bird shit on their caps. "Bliss Brass" always ensured that they had more rows of gold on their caps than their provincial policing counterparts. Harold was an officer of distinction. The forge cap would remain on his head until such time that he went inside a dwelling. Upon entering a dwelling, Harold would remove the cap promptly and without hesitation. It would be placed precisely against the left side of his torso. Yet another, much bigger rule book contained the grooming and clothing secrets. This rule book specified that the cap was to be removed at no less than a 60 degree angle. Sergeant Bernie, not to be outdone, had a police cap too. Sadly, his cap looked ever so bleak against the back drop of Harold's gold leaf. Earl knew that the boss wouldn't be much for small talk, so the old staff took up the lead.

Earl spoke up in a very friendly but noticeably contrived tone, "Sir, good to see you. How was the autumn drive? Really nice colors on the trees!" In theory, there was no way that a comment like that could be negatively received. It was, after all, transmitted from the heart and sprinkled ever so lightly with sarcastic insincerity.

Earl looked at Harold's eyes through the superintendent's regulation wired rimmed glasses. There were two distinct areas of glass lens separating the bifocals. Progressive lenses came at a much greater expense and were considered by District as an optional visual aid. Harold sported his dress white shirt complete with the appropriate badges and time in the rank insignia. Like a friend sizing up your sister, Earl gazed his boss up and down. Earl couldn't help but think that there might be a little bit of baked potato still clinging to his right shoulder pip. If he could only get Mushy to aim Licit at that shoulder flash, we could have some real action!

It was obvious to Earl that Kate was trying her very best to avoid the situation unfolding before her eyes. The staff contemplated her constant leg shifting, as indicative of tension operating in conjunction with a heightened "pee factor." Given the opulence of the moment and no music to accompany the "Grand March," there remained an ever cloaking stillness. In the distance, the stage was set, the rubber dog toy loudly bouncing again off Licit's head. The distant thud spontaneously redirected the group's attention.

Earl looked on at the bouncing rubber toy and contemplated how it was just like a dog to simply "be a dog" during a period of extended human tension. For a moment, Earl felt strangely compelled to grab Harold's gold brimmed hat and fire it into the air for Licit's delight. As if his mind was hard drive partitioned, he made a mental note for inclusion on the "get even list."

Superintendent Thompson was the first one to crack the silence after Earl's opening remarks. It was now 4:30 P.M. There would only be an hour or so of daylight. In terms of a hotel, there wasn't much in Hill Mountain. Like most Manitoba towns, there were the classic four hotel rooms either in back or on top of the beverage room. If you believed the Liquor Commission, all four of these rooms were supposed to be rentable. In reality, the band and the owner each had a room reserved for cocaine blows. Best case scenario, there would be two available rooms. Furthermore, there was virtually no chance that any of the rooms would have two windows. Bunking up would have to be the norm if the crew was to spend the night. It was either Hill Mountain or back to Rolicking. Of course, some worker bees would have to hang by the scene and guard it through the night. Worse case, you locked the doors to the Co-op and hoped that the next morning would not introduce additional body parts.

Harold asked, "Is there any place we can talk and brief ourselves?"

Earl thought to himself that he had never heard "brief ourselves" used in that context. It seemed somewhat odd but remarkably Harold at the same time. Earl enjoyed taking note of management's expressions. He would jot them down then try to work them into a future memo. Shit, brief ourselves sounded almost pervertingly plausible.

Kate responded silently to Harold while stepping up to the political plate. She gestured with her chin in an upwards direction indicating Mom's. In reality it was Mom's or the bar. There was once a small RCP patrol cabin in Hill Mountain but due to rodent infiltration it was finally condemned. The descriptor "cabin" is typically reserved for a premise that is, in some small way, fit for human habitation. The Department had let the trailer run down, not so much out of intent but out of a more perverse sense of reckless abandon. Even in its prime, the trailer was seldom used by the Rolicking Rural Members. It had always been kept on the roster for a crime scene which simply never transpired.

Briefings especially at the beginning of an investigation were always mandatory. The logic of the police briefing was to try and prevent cops from spinning totally out of control. The premise was well founded in the Bliss Landing Operational Manual. It was also rooted within the investigational procedural annals of way smarter cops. Police work by its very nature was always linked at the hip by policies of those cops way smarter than the current subset. Often, policy was so old no one really remembered how it originated. With the passing of time, procedural etiquette was accepted as a norm rather than an historical suggestion.

Young cops always quoted chapter and verse from policy as if it was truly "biblical" in proportion. The truth be known, most good cops simply led by the same guiding principles that always worked in the past. Earl was the best example of a trial and error cop. The troops always knew that Earl represented the right path because the old staff had, at one point or another—crawled down all the wrong paths.

The investigational circle initiated their stroll over to Mom's. Harold took up the lead while Sergeant Bernie opened the squeaking metal door. Earl could not help but simply look on and shake his weary head. He thought to himself that if overtime came up in the discussion, he would have to hold himself back. The troops were now well along on the gravy train. No choice, Earl always liked to consider himself a pragmatic manager. From his point of view, money is quite simply reduced to the buying power of time. If the troops worked, they got paid.

The police parade wandered back to the same waiting booth in the back. The noon hour crowd had long since departed the hula show. There was the usual point of indecision as to who should sit where. Who would be fortunate enough to grab the wall side of the booth? It wasn't as if you could pull up a chair. Seating was fixed. You were either going to booth it or lunch counter it, "Chez Mom's." Earl made damn sure that he sat across from Harold. In the overall battle plan, the rook could be sacrificed to capture a queen. He would politely let his boss grab the wall and he would counter his move accordingly. To lose first choice was just fine if, in the end, you conquered a more gratifying tactical position.

Kate was first in one side of the booth and plunked herself beside a window. Earl sat down immediately beside her. This was best case scenario. Although there was only Earl and Kate on one side of the booth, Earl's butt width absorbed all the remaining seating space. There had been other meetings where Kate was known to sit across from Earl. She would wiggle her ears and nose in mindless play. It was childish shit, absolutely! In the big scheme, shit that turned the hours of work into pensionable years.

Earl looked at Thompson who didn't even have the savvy to sit at the end of the booth. He sat across and jammed in the middle between Sergeant Bernie and Mushy. His pips clinging to his shoulder flashes were heaved up tight against his neck. They rode up so high that they could have easily been mistaken for big round disco earrings. It wasn't really Harold's fault. Mushy had, more or less, turned to him and offered up the obvious set up. Mushy was not without his own style of employment humor. Appositionally speaking, things could not be any better for the old staff. Kate picked up the police radio and tried P.B. He answered the call and was en route over to Mom's.

Earl wondered to himself just where the hell P.B. was going to sit. In fact, all the booths in Mom's were more physically suited for four than five. With Kate by the window, he would have to sandwich P.B. in the middle or take the center hit himself. He picked up the salt shaker and started playing with it. Brown grains of rice could be seen floating on top of the salt. He took the old glass shaker by the top and shook the bottom. It was if the rice was permanently affixed to the surface. A thought blazoned across Earl's mind—what if it wasn't brown rice?

P.B. walked into Mom's and stared down at the auspicious table. P.B. acknowledged the small group and looked briefly around. He had his notebook in one hand and a brief case in the other. P.B. checked out his options. There were several stain ridden high chairs stacked in the entrance way to the washrooms. Clearly, this option was ruled out. Earl made a valiant attempt to move closer to Kate but his ass cheek could only carve out another two inches. P.B. shrugged as if to acknowledge his fate and chose a stool directly across from the booth. Earl took positive note and gave P.B. an approving wink. The wink of Earl could mean many things. In this case, it simply was intended to transmit approval. The stool was obviously a much better choice than the floor adjacent to Earl's ass.

* * * *

Kate was particularly adept at sensing a distinct imbalance of testosterone in any room. She thought to herself that it was not so much imbalance but the greater stupidity of males at play. Sure, women played games too. However, the male of the species was always "on game." She always knew it to be the unspoken rule that a woman must always break any male dominated silence. Someday she planned to have a rule book herself filled with the collective wisdom of enlightened chick cops. Kate had learned from experience that dangling male hormones would only fuel negative consequence.

She turned to her extreme left side and addressed P.B. who was now tactically distanced from the booth. Kate was hungry as all hell. Her tummy growls had revealed the secret. She would kill for a cinnamon bun right now! She leaned around Earl and asked P.B., "Did we get anywhere with the witness interviews?"

P.B. sat up on the stool and opened up his notebook. He looked directly at Harold and replied, "Sir, I've interviewed two residents of Hill Mountain that were asleep last night. There is no indication that anything unusual transpired at the store in question. I canvassed all residents in the area and there are no known CCTV cameras. No one has seen McIvor since late yesterday."

* * * *

Earl immediately picked up on the fact that P.B. had looked away from Kate. The old staff thought to himself, the asshole must figure he has the Bliss job all wrapped up. Too bad, I kind of liked the kid. Like a drummer working the pedal, Earl could feel Kate's left knee moving up and down. She was obviously keenly aware that P.B. had seized the moment at her expense. Earl chuckled to himself. P.B. is going to pay the price with Kate—dumb fucker.

Most senior managers are never content with the status quo. Good police work requires fine attention to detail. The worst case scenario is that you run over detail at the expense of speed. Speed really isn't required with police work unless there is an exterior driver like a serial killer or politically injected haste. The severed hand was simply not going anywhere fast. It would just be Earl's luck if, by chance, the hand had crawled away.

Superintendent Thompson raised his torso in the cramped booth. He tried to move both arms but they were otherwise jammed in tight to his sides. Mushy would clearly not give ground. If anything the dog handler pushed harder on the wall which, in turn, crunched him even tighter into Harold. The superintendent managed to free his right arm by slightly dipping his left shoulder. Earl glanced across at his boss. Mushy looked out the window at the doggie truck while picking at his teeth with a plastic stir stick. Kate stared at P.B. who himself, remained fixed on the biggest boss in the middle.

Harold cleared his voice while simultaneously moving his right arm. It was as if the arm was somehow disconnected at the shoulder. He could flail it only from the elbow while moving it marginally in noticeable discomfort. In a perfect world, Sergeant Bernie at the aisle should have given up some space but he remained fixated on the hula girl. Her grass skirt swirled as she spoke of almost 5:00 P.M. The show was most appropriately, closed for the day.

Harold spoke up, "I feel that we need to set the investigation in motion with the utmost diligence. It is clearly unacceptable that this killing is going on in our jurisdiction without appropriate challenge. The Confinement Team is en route. We have a missing man and a suspect limb. I take it, that we can at least find the man."

Earl stared on at his boss. He wanted desperately to fill in the blank looks with a, "What the fuck?" Mushy bit down hard on the plastic stick. Licit barked outside the restaurant. Kate's leg continued to pedal out some major tune. Sergeant Bernie remained targeted to his hula friend. In a manner resembling a spring fixed headed animal on a '68 Bug dashboard, P.B. nodded his head up and down in silent approval.

There is a point in every cop's life where someone will witness a cop commit a crime. It may be as insignificant as a stapler off the head or a conductive energy shot in a double latté. At some point, it is bound to happen. When it does happen, the unabridged version of the rule book dictates that you maintain absolute deniability. In the back of a restaurant there was no sense of deniability. It either happened in front of you and you noticed, or you were struck down blind. Some cops might lean over and tie a shoe but to bend down in a small booth—an unlikely option.

As if seizing fate for what it was, Mushy turned to his immediate extreme right and propelled the plastic stir stick into Superintendent Harold Thompson's face. Because Mushy was somewhat higher in physical stature, the stick struck dead center to the boss' forehead. It was not a hit lacking DNA. It was served "au jus" with Mushy slobber. The stick remained briefly in suspension. It then dropped to Harold's lap and tumbled under the booth.

P.B. stood up from his stool. It was almost as if he had planned to dive under the table and recover the assault weapon. Although, there was part of Earl that would have liked to see P.B. hit the dirt, he motioned him to sit back down. Kate's leg had somehow been vanquished of constant motion.

Sergeant Bernie looked briefly sideways to Harold then refocused on his Hawaiian delight.

Mushy had never been accused of being a slouch with imagination. He simply opened his eyes to their fullest, tossed his head back and offered up for suggestion, "Geez, Sir my apologies—bad habit on my part. Are you okay?"

Earl winked at Mushy. It was more of a tightly closed eye flicker than an actual wink. The tension had been sufficiently rebutted by a stir stick. It was not the prose that would ever win accolades but nevertheless, a very inspiring cue. Earl picked up the same cue and chalked it up while eyeballing his one arm opponent across the booth. The old staff thought to himself that it would be a little like kicking a puppy. Maybe he should just reach under the table and grab the old man by his rebar. Having weighed out the plausible options, it just did not feel right to trump Mushy's moment. Earl wiggled both of his arms while Kate gave up the necessary ground.

* * * *

Kate had seen it all over the years. If Earl simply popped the boss in the eye she would see absolutely nothing. The detective could easily tell Internal Affairs that she was totally focused on not wetting her pants—gotta pee, could not see. Eyes were much easier to evade than ears. Kate secretly hoped if Earl said anything bad, that it was something that rhymed with something good. Like "ass hole" and "crass fellow" something like that…. There could always be different renderings of verbiage.

Earl smirked at the superintendent like he had done on dozens of occasions. There was that overwhelming post coital tension that draped over the coffee shop. The old staff said, "Confinement Team great idea! We need some uniforms for the scene and it would have cost me big bucks to bring them in from Rolicking. Confinement, is after all, a District tab. The City of Rolicking salutes you Sir!"

Chapter 18
Yes, We Have No Command Post

The decision was mutually reached to try and obtain suitable "investigational facilities" at the local hotel. There was only one hotel in Hill Mountain. It was represented by the local beverage room which also doubled as the proverbial community meeting place. Many of the locals frequented the establishment in pursuit of those ever evasive high card winnings. The hotel was aptly named "The Royal Flush." The outside marquee divulged the fact that the word "Flush" had been added to the name around the same time that video lottery terminals were introduced. Any passerby could easily see the failed attempt at matching prior script with the new word "Flush." The owner and operator Bob McTavish worked the beer vendor, mini restaurant and bar. There was the expected amount of inordinate juggling. Bob and his wife Agnes had been operating the place for decades.

The team of scientists now worked the exterior of the Co-op. They sported the latest in forensic fall fashion. Completing the look in Milan and, breaking the Labor Day rule, was a matching white bunny suit with complimentary cotton slippers. The goal is always the preservation of evidence through the practice of exacting standards. The scientists' job would entail the meticulous piecing of evidentiary samples into something far more tangible. It was far from a perfect scene. The surrounding area along the back of the Co-op was obviously very well travelled. Earl and Kate had themselves contaminated the scene through their preliminary verification.

P.B. stood in the lobby of the hotel with Sergeant Bernie and Harold. Mushy, Earl and Kate loosely guarded the scene. Hanging with the utmost authority, the Health Department sign now looked like it fully belonged. It was now a Manitoba Fall, 6:15 P.M. and it was damn dark. This made it a very bad scene for physically searching but an excellent scene for the "Zap Light." The Zap Light was an ultraviolet, wattage induced, digitally ionized, wonder beam that the scientists regularly used in their duties. Ironically, the problem with the process is that it can very well shed too much light on a dark scene. With the introduction of luminal, bodily fluids canine or otherwise could easily brighten up the Manitoba night. At the end of the day, it becomes a very subjective exercise, as to what DNA is reasonably foreign.

Bliss Landing Ident travelled with every piece of equipment known to mankind. All the tools of the trade were housed in road ready tough cases that could be transported anywhere. Earl and Kate helped Ident set up the massive "Hollywood" lights that now torched up the night. This would certainly attract some local attention. That's it, nice cover. The Health Department is filming a Public Service Announcement. Earl speculated that he just might have to garnish a clapboard and dawn a beret. He would have to fire up yet another sign, "Closed Set: Movie in Production."

Mushy sat in his truck and Licit snored in the back. The troops had heard little from Rolicking since Harold arrived. Earl knew that the whole town would eventually realize the situation and the jig would be up. Whether it mattered or not, remained to be seen. It's not as if a major news crew would suddenly show up in Hill Mountain or was it? The media could not be controlled; they had to be effectively managed. Earl had some history with T.V. He had at one point or another dangled all the wrong participles in public.

There was no primary media spokesperson for the Department. Earl had some very basic training in the finer art of "non-speak." which was the RCP language of choice. As long as your media target was satisfied that they heard something tangible—the delivery boy was off the hook. Earl had learned the hard way that it was way better to state, "We have a suspicious scene and are in the process of linking aspects of this investigation to other innate discrepancies" as opposed to, "We have a big problem, we have spent far too much money and there are body parts everywhere." The differences in media disclosure, be they ever so subtle, can severely compromise an investigation. In Earl's mind, there was one positive good that could be derived from Harold's presence in Hill Mountain—tag you are it! Sure, the boss could always deflect the media to Earl but would he? Once Hill Mountain was invaded by those that wrote to link murders would Harold pick up the torch and consequently, the microphone?

Earl and Kate maintained a healthy distance from Ident. In a perfect world there would be at least eight uniformed Rolicking officers at the scene. This is where police reality and fiction parted company. There was no cop power left in Rolicking to handle both the end of the month pay cycle "happenings" and yet another crime scene. The Confinement Team was not total over load. Once the Team arrived they could guard the scene pending any further developments. This was not a typical Confinement Team call out. There was no desperado barricaded with a gun, no warrant to apprehend and most certainly, no child lying deep in a well.

Earl felt certain that Confinement would arrive decked out in camo and commando style makeup. They too travelled with very high tech equipment which included but was not limited to pneumatic battering rams, night vision binoculars, laser weapon sights, strobe flashlights, gas launchers, stun grenades, flash sticks and yes, overtime forms. It was okay though, because the Team was actually funded from a collective body of dollars paid for by District.

Earl lit up another cigarette. He never smoked this much when he was busy. The scientists had grown sensitive to light and they turned immediately to acknowledge their disapproval. Nothing worse than that space suit glare— it is right up there with the third cup stare. With the dexterity of a fire plug, Earl immediately turned his body to the opposite direction. Earl looked at Kate and asked somewhat rhetorically, "Is it just me or have we been standing here all day?"

Kate replied, "Yes we have, and although I eventually had a leak, it would seem strangely … that I have to go again. Mom's is now closed and I'm going to head over the hotel soon. Oh ya, my other girly issue is still not resolved. I'm having a swell time!"

It was the best part about Kate she remained an eternal realist at the worst of times. She had obviously coped with the sanitary tribulations of the day and was the better person for it. Kate had a lot of energy but Earl could see that she was worn out. They had been spinning wheels all day with absolutely no progress. Any cop will tell you that it's always tougher to wait and do squat than actually work. So much in policing was geared to next move—wait. The next move was seldom unwanted, even at its worse it was always greeted with relief.

So far the weather had cooperated. It was still bone dry but the wind from the west was blowing in change. The weather forecast was light rain overnight. In all certainty, this would mean a torrential down pour. Rain would wreak havoc on both the scene and tracking. Ident knew that whatever chance they had at a scene would likely only last for several hours. It would not be the first crime scene that had been tarped for days. Once there were fresh troops, they would construct a tent over as much of the exterior as possible. A tarp would not keep ground moisture from percolating into the scene. The tarp wasn't an absolute fix but given the conditions, it was the best fix possible.

* * * *

Kate saw the bright headlights of the Confinement Team bus as it bounced into town. There was absolutely no sense of it arriving from the distance. The bus was seemingly vaporized into the night. There was a fine fog in the evening air where the cooler night air hit the still warm October ground. It wasn't exactly a fog but more aptly, a hovering mist that hung two feet off the ground. The bus' large size looked remarkably out of context given the confines of the small town. The Team rode fully prepared to wage war. The Confinement Team represented those cops that moved and breathed as one. They could easily weather it out in the Manitoba night. The members of the Team were handpicked from a group of volunteers. Those that eagerly sought out the intrinsic rewards associated with a higher calling to ninja style policing.

She didn't quite get the whole notion. In fact, she really wrote it all off to boys with toys. It's not that she didn't like to have them around—quite the contrary. They were certainly a divergence from the classic RCP fall fashion lineup. The soldiers looked damn good in camo which combined ever so lightly with the "je ne sais quoi" scent of gun oil. The intensity associated with the Team was second only to premenstrual cramps. Kate continued to look at the headlight's beam. The glow displaced erratically in the mist. In every other detail, it was otherwise a very non-descript bus. There was no marquee on the side of the bus introducing the Team. The bus had been retrofitted nicely to suit the subtlety of clandestine missions. Confinement was now operating on a local police channel. They could fully communicate with the Rolicking officers.

The Team Commander was one, Sergeant Phillip Rothersay. He should have been a media man with the initials "P.R." Instead, he best personified a lava breathing commando cop summoned up from the bowels of hell. Kate was quite certain that his blood ran far cooler than any other cop. If you looked real close you could see his white fangs in the night. "Team Leader" had those chiseled facial looks of a male stripper but a body that better expressed a diligence to pastry. He was tough but rubber tough, in a way that evoked more respect than fear. Phillip was the kind of cop that could unassumingly throw a bowling ball while simultaneously slicing an adversary's throat. If you believe legends, Rothersay was known to carry one fragmenting bowling ball and six "just in case" knives on his person.

Mushy was once again outside with Licit. He had him on leash and was going out back of Mom's for an overdue evening wiz. The dog spun while barking at the oncoming bus. He stared at the big tires like they were giant rubber toys. The minute that bus stopped, Mushy had made up his mind to let Licit piss all over the big tires.

Kate held up her portable radio and listened, "Superintendent Thompson— Team Leader Rothersay, Superintendent Thompson."

Harold responded, "Go Ahead Team Leader."

Team Leader said, "We have a visual of the situation. Request permission to park our mobilization vehicle and deploy."

There was a brief pause. Harold stuttered into his portable, "You have permission to park." There was dead silence. Mushy was now beside Kate and Earl. The dog handler's presence had created the seed of a small circle.

Earl ended the silence, "I guess first things first; makes sense. First we park the bus then we deploy. I mean, it's not like you could do it the other way around, right...?"

Mushy looked back at Earl. He puffed long and hard on the old staff's comments. He injected, "They are not trained to think like us. You have to tell them in stages. Really ... it is a damn good idea or all hell would break loose."

Kate also seized the moment to fire in her two cents, "In fact, I might add, Harold should have clarified exactly where they should park the damn bus. Our good Team Leader also screwed up by not articulating the GPS coordinates of said parking spot."

With that prevailing sentiment, the air brakes sounded and the bus dipped forward to a final stop. Through the tinted windows Kate could see the shadowy movement of black figures. Vague, not yet distinguishable outlines, stirred inside the bus causing it to violently shake. All that Kate could think about was the toilet on the bus. Sure, it would stink of "boy" but at least she could shut the damn door. Earl and Mushy stood closely together watching the scene unfold. The old man that Kate had seen earlier staggered out from under the bridge. He must have heard the big bus and wondered what the hell was going on. Small town Manitoba after 8:00 P.M. was, for the most part, all rolled up for the night. Hill Mountain should be no different. Tonight was the exception. It would give local folks coffee talk for days.

The door of the bus opened and Sergeant Rothersay exited while several other Team members spread out along the street. His camo pants were tightly packed into the tops of his laced black combat boots. His flak jacket was adorned with the military tools of the trade. The Team members exited slowly, simultaneously one by one—demonstrating excessive precision. They sported ear pieces and wrap around microphones which evoked a "spaceman" like quality. They had their issued .308's complete with laser sights. Like the anticipation of Christmas coming, several of the Team members peeped excitedly through their night scopes. Good thing Mom didn't step out because she would have been aglow with red dots. Keying their portable radios, communication checks were completed by Team Leader with each of the other Confinement Team members. In predefined sequence, Team members one through ten confirmed radio reception. Members eleven and twelve were noticeably absent—papa leave.

The Confinement Team was geared to "the ready." The reins were pulled tight and spurs flashed sparks in the night. Earl watched Sergeant Rothersay come towards them with his tinted night vision visor in place. Kate leaned to Earl and whispered, "His opening line has to be, take me to your leader."

* * * *

Phillip Rothersay approached Earl and the group. While moving closer, he lifted his visor and surprisingly, exchanged greetings. Kate soared over to the bus to take better command of Mother Nature. Philip replaced the helmet with a more appropriate floppy army hat. Team Leader then pulled the hat cord slider tightly under his chin. The old staff made a note to himself, "Put whistle on Rothersay's hat string."

Earl remained glued to the camo garb, high tech equipment, stun grenades, gloves and most likely Kevlar gitch. He thought to himself, nothing like a District budget. Now that the Team was here, Kate and Earl could grab some rest. First step would be to check out the situation at the hotel. Maybe they got lucky and the band didn't show. Kind of funny if the coke blowers saw the army and flushed their product! It wouldn't be the first time that a stash was dumped in the ensuing anxiety of a spontaneous police presence.

Earl arranged with Phillip to take up control of the scene. There were the usual entry log books that somehow didn't seem to fit the otherwise low volume traffic situation. The log book served as the official record of who entered the scene along with date, time, and specific purpose. Crime scene management was long past the point of the senior rank simply strolling in to "gawk" at blood. Movement in and out of a crime scene often resulted in a downstream issue in court. The evolution of DNA had also brought about the defense of cross contamination. In fact, it was the investigation most times and not the accused that was actually on trial. Earl picked up the ledger and jotted down their departure at 9:38 P.M.

The night air was now brisk, damp and much colder. Earl was glad that he had worn a sports jacket. However, he would have much preferred his old bush jacket. Earl turned to Kate, "Listen I got no intention of staying here with that fucking crew. Let's go to the cabin and come back in the morning. I'll just run it by the old man." Harold was in fact, much younger than Earl but in the old staff's mind it was rank that bumped him to the moniker of *old man*. Kate and Earl walked across the main drag and into the hotel. Earl took a minute to acknowledge pleasantries with Bob McTavish.

The old staff bought a couple of small bags of ketchup chips and two orange sodas. He smiled like the father of new puppies and proudly presented his offering to Kate. There was really no choice. It was either ketchup chips or cheesies. It was culinary simplicity at its finest. No arguing the merit of raspberry vinaigrette over a Catalina dressing. Food, was by all admissions, far too much on the go these days. Diet and an approaching size 14 be damned, Kate gladly engulfed the chips and soda. It was accompanied with the primal delight associated with finding something delectable to eat. The detective thought for a minute about the shopping trip to Bliss that simply never happened. There would be other occasions to shop. An evening bag of ketchup chips, a delicacy—best preserved in memory. Kate peered into the bag and there sat, plastic wrapped and gleaming in the fluorescent light; a voucher for a free bag of chips.

Chapter 19
The Trap Line

Rookie Ron Fleury was lucky and got the time off before all hell broke loose in Hill Mountain. Once the sergeant had called him he jumped at the chance to get a free ride to the city. He was still seeing his High School sweetie who was in the process of relocating to the North. She was a teacher in Winnipeg and was actively scoping jobs out in Rolicking. Ron's mind wandered while he bounced up and down the heaving pavement. The sports car's suspension couldn't help but creak out the odd mechanical objection. Foot deep drops were not uncommon on the road surface. It was rough now, but once the ice hit, a low slung car would be out of the question.

Ron didn't know much about vintage wheels. In his mind, vehicles stopped and started with the latest gadgetry. Ron was the product of an air included, satellite cranked up, wash and wear, ready to rock generation. He was an urban player now, through and through. He had taken the job in Rolicking simply because both money and opportunity were excellent. He was originally from the North but he had grown up in Winnipeg with a foster family. He had every intention of going back to civilization just as soon as a bigger police department knocked.

The RCP was good for his résumé. He would definitely prove an asset to another police agency down the road. He didn't want to end up a bush cop like Mike or Earl. He thought to himself how cynical and belittling they all were. It was almost as if they were somehow energized by inner office conflict. Who really gives a fuck about a dirty shirt in the big picture? Someday Ron thought, I'll have to tell the staff that he went down a notch on that shot. I'm a damn hard working guy. The boss behind the window should reasonably know that I would change my shirt. Do they think that I want to look like a damn geek? Maybe I should just launch an office harassment allegation. No, that would blow up in my face for sure.

Earl just came on way too strong. He had tons of great qualities and he knew the Department's policies inside and out. There was no one in the office but Kate that could equal him with those chippy low rising slap shots. Earl really had two sides. He could be a very nice guy, but there were other times when he obviously chose to asshole out.

There was stimulating office banter but there was also the crossover stuff. It angered Ron to think about the shot about the dirty shirt. You would think that they never had a beginning. It's not easy at the beginning, they just forget. Twenty years ago policing was a walk in the park. Why can't they just see how tough it is for us? It wasn't my generation that invented these computer systems that don't work worth shit. No, no ... but we're expected to link them all up and then solve crime?

Ron reflected on the six different types of data banks that existed in the Department. None of these systems could ever begin to cyber-chat with each other. It was similar to a rocket launch where separate engineers build the rockets. Geez, I wonder why the hell the damn thing won't fly straight? Earl always talked about the amalgamation with District as a crushing blow to the Department. Ron shrugged to himself. It had all evolved far before his time. Earl liked to talk about the past, about a blanket warrant called a "Writ of Assistance." Apparently, this was a "pre-Charter" phenomenon which allowed certain designated cops to search at will. Ron at his early age could certainly understand the potential for abuse.

The young cop knew that sooner or later he would catch a big break. It was simply a matter of merging luck with the fate of a good investigation. He caught a break tonight, a paid trip to the city! Some cops happen by good files and other officers can never catch a deuce. Although he was fresh out of the Academy, Ron knew that he could make early promotional Vindication. He just needed the opportunity to kick ass. He could rise above them all. It was just a matter of waiting things out and then making it happen. He hoped that he would never be called to a crap file like the break in at the florist.

If he could be only half as good as Mike but maintain some semblance of control, things would be fine. Ron speculated that the key to working with management is not to confront them but creatively steer around them. You couldn't suck hole to a guy like Earl. You can target his rough edges and shave them off day by day.

The big bosses decided all the positions for the ICU jobs. To be on their bad list would certainly be counterproductive. Management wasn't really Harold or Earl it was simply that intangible opposing force. Ron had worked in a big box store in Winnipeg there was management there too. The difference was police managers had "zero sense" of delivery. They dished out big portions of abuse with every negatively inspired sentiment. The RCP had cyber grown to the point where most of the abuse was emails. No percentage really, why even log fucking in? Email messages adorned with sarcastic innuendo were just too easily blasted out. A snotty message sent by Earl could severely trash morale all night. For some intangible, gladiator equated rationale, guns and emails simply didn't feel right. Would the Emperor have sent Spartacus an email criticizing his day with the lions?

Ron could not remember the last time that the brass did something decent for the cops on the floor. Although you were entitled to order new pants, just try to sneak the damn form past Earl. Was he the fucking regimental seamstress or what? It was like the boss was spending his own money. Ron felt his face flush as he grew angry in the rainy night drive.

He picked up his silvery travel mug and sipped at his now cold coffee. There was no way to prevent his mind from wandering. Everyone lost critical focus on these long and boring trips. Could it be simply, "Oh look, I'm passing another tree. Hope I didn't lose count!" For a fleeting moment, Ron thought about his past life. It was long ago now and perhaps better not remembered. At same time, the constable noticed a rain drop hit the crack free windshield. He would try to keep the rocks from spidering the glass but it was an inevitable Manitoba risk. A cracked windshield in the North was like snot in the cold—bound to happen, hard and ugly.

Ron straightened up his posture and tried to refocus on the evening cruise. Once it got dark it was far too easy to smack a moose. A sports car provided no real protection from a major impact. The rotary engine in the car was far quieter than anything he had ever driven. It had severe juice. He stared down at the white envelope on the passenger seat. Mike had given him $1000.00 cash for gas down and a plane ride back. Mike was a solid guy. He wasn't even that pushy about receipts for the trip. Ron wondered just how much coin Mike raked in with the restoration business.

Sergeant Mike was the kind of guy that knew it all. Whether it be welding or fabricating he could modify or create just about anything. Ron had contemplated the possibility of working with Mike and maybe picking up some extra money and skills. This was the second time that he had thrown him car keys for the city. The last one was an old '65 New Yorker. Like a fat date at last call, very comfortable, but the ride was more like cruising on a couch than driving something hot!

The RX-7 was a real machine. The young constable pushed the pedal down hard. There would be no cops along the highway until Bliss. He turned on the radio and he was relieved to hear satellite. He was glad he brought the MP3. Just in case the satellite signal faded in the rain. Most folks figure that a cop can drive any speed they want. It's simply not the case. You have to always look out. Hell, there were cops outside the RCP that would "major league" relish in doing their own. He looked around the car in the darkness and admired the new seats. The sergeant never explained how he got into the business. It must have just been there. I guess he seized the moment. The young cop respected the sergeant's work ethic. There's a solid guy who didn't waste his days off watching the tube. The smooth leather seats made the interior smell new again. Ron thought, so much in life, is work served back with a double shot of chance.

There would be no construction delays en route. This was the only perk of driving at night. Ron kind of felt a little sad. He had run into Ashley Funk several times the past summer and they seemed to hit it off. The good sergeant would have had his pigeon toed ass if he found out. The one thing that Ron truly despised about Rolicking was the talk. Who you fucked and who fucked you was town business. He had run into Ashley several times in the local bars. It was hard to make a move on the boss' daughter with all the other cops around. One thing he had to watch out for was his girlfriend in Winnipeg strolling haphazardly into the RCP trap line. He had known guys that even got burned at Winnipeg airport. Manitoba was really that small. You had to expect to get torched, flushed and spit on. Once you accept nature's decreed plan, all that's left is creating a softer landing. The trick in ultimate male survival is to always have a plan. A bad plan is better than no plan at all. Ron knew that he was now at the point of crucial decision making. You can only lay down so many traps before your prey crisscross and tear out a throat.

His girlfriend Rachel in Winnipeg had not come up to visit. Ron had made every effort to dissuade her. This necessarily meant that Mohammad must now travel south to the mountain. This was by all means, not a perfect plot. She could surprise him; knife in mouth at any point! Deep down inside, Ron knew that this would be his inevitable fate. Once in Rolicking, Rachel would be targeted by the other wives and girlfriends who would then administer the sacred ceremony.

Ron envisioned the future happening. The presence of cookies, dainties and tea would not serve to undermine intent. The conversation would evolve as per the scripted plan, "Welcome to Rolicking Dear, these are surveillance shots of your boyfriend with the sergeant's daughter. They were taken with a "Monoco 100" night vision scope at 150 yards. Resistance is futile, please drink from the collector cup of social harmony. You are now one of us."

The odd thing was … he did not consider himself a player. The really sleazy players always seemed to be self preserved with an intrinsic sense of immunity. He wasn't particularly good looking but passable good looks was all that a guy needed in Rolicking. The rest of the hunt was piecing the package together. Last call is all about the sales pitch and not the final product.

He remembered seeing Ashley in the bar with "8 Ball." He secretly wanted to tell Mike—God damn it, he must have known. The whole town did. Those drug dealers should just leave the cops' families out of the equation. It should always be, what always has been, cops on one side of the bar and hoods on the other.

Ron muddled over his social analysis. He concluded, chicks attracted to dollars, that's all. The bad guys have more money than most cops so they naturally controlled the local "action." There was the notable exception to the rule. Not all the locals targeted guys with coin. There were others that focused on a ready-made family situation. Ron wanted no part of paternity leave quite yet. He remembered how there used to be eight cops that regularly did up the bars and now there were but four. Can't guys see this daddy thing coming? One minute at the shooter bar and the next in diapers. What the fuck happened here? Maybe a guy's ultimate destiny simply evolves from early childhood development. Blanket sporting chicks in bars inevitably transgress to babies in blankets. Another round please—this one's on Darwin.

Ron looked down at the portable radio on the passenger seat. Although cell service was much better now, most cops took a portable radio just in case. Ron had decided to bring his service weapon. In his mind, he had developed a very keen sense of survival. Young cops had it all over the old ones in the tactical game. Sure the old ones were still around, the ultimate proof of survival but they had absolutely no defensive edge. He lifted the console lid and peeked into the felt lined interior. He had to make damn sure he didn't leave his 9 mm behind. Ron took a moment to peer at the gun. It looked kind of neat—the fluorescent front sight glowed piss yellow in the night.

* * * *

Mike Funk paced his living room clutching a coffee. He had entrusted the RX-7 to Fleury. The young cop fit the role nicely. He was instructed to drive to Winnipeg and bring the car to a precise address in the North end. The rush for the trip was spun out of greater economic urgency. The car had to be flipped over to a business associate early the next morning.

The sergeant gazed out his living room window. He was one of the lucky ones in town who had bought a house with a view. He had no neighbors across the street, only a snowmobile trail. His comings and goings could only be scrutinized by his neighbors to the side. There wasn't any snow yet but quad traffic burned up the muddy trails until winter arrived. In the darkness, he could hear the engines roar under the throttle crank of avid enthusiasts.

Mike was alone in the house. Ashley was out again. It wasn't that bad now that 8 Ball was gone. Mike hoped that there would never be another gangster. Deep down inside, he knew that that was easier said than done. She was at the age where the sergeant really didn't want to know everything but quite likely did. She had snuck into bars and as expected, some of the cops dropped not so subtle hints. Mike wondered why the fuck they didn't tell her to get her young ass home. The answer was obvious but at the same time insatiable to any dad—the boys wanted her around. She was outgoing and good looking the worst possible combination for any father. She was 16 and just a little older than most of her girlfriends. The trouble was 16 is backseat legal.

The old sergeant thought back to the night under the bridge. Maybe it could have ended differently, it really didn't matter now. He felt a little bad about the 9 mm barrel. There was simply no other way. It boiled down to a matter of family priority. He had chosen one of the spare 9 mm's from the exhibit locker. If the incident was ever investigated there would simply be a bullet with no history. After all, history survives in the barrel of the weapon. Fleury's new weapon posed no challenge. The barrel was switched with the spare 9 mm. The weapon was now clean. It looked like it never needed a wash. If need be, a barrel could be switched multiple times and then eventually tossed. A different part on a RCP gun was really not a big deal. Over the years several 9 mm's were retrofitted with new barrels, grips and triggers. Let's face it, any weapon represents but a macro machine of smaller parts. There was really no such thing as any "gun" being a murder weapon. The barrel of a 9 mm introduces the epilogue not the prologue. The only conclusive proof of actual fire was divulged by the lands and grooves in the barrel. If the tattoos on a person reveal character, then the barrel of a gun flashed her tattoos most discreetly inside.

Sergeant Funk still remembered the druggie's final plea. It was quick—there was supposed to be more talk. Mike was not in the business of inflicting pain—the stapler thing just happened. There is a distinct difference between impulsive anger and intentional cruelty. 8 Ball could have simply left town. It could have easily ended there. There was no need to tune in McIvor. It was contained at that point. He could have better handled the situation. In the end there was little choice, McIvor had to go. The drops at the Co-op and the florist were finely tuned. Packages of product got picked up and moved into Rolicking. Conversely, money flowed back steady to the city. Of course, some money did stay in the North. 8 Ball should have known that the rules of the game demanded control. His family was always off limits. The old sergeant tolerated the hood's prior shakedown of McIvor but Ashley was a fatal mistake.

Its odd how there was so much money to be made yet there still remained uncontrolled greed. There was a distinct sense of perversion enshrouded in fucking arrogance. Sergeant Funk surmised that there was always a reason for the game to end. Mike wondered to himself if he too was at the beginning or end of play. The rules had been made up on the fly—the scoreboard long gone. He could live with the rumor mill but he had no intention of Ashley co-existing with disgusting town talk. If he was gone what would Ashley do? She was more than capable of flipping out the other way. There would always be more 8 Balls.

The suspension had created some logistical problems. He still had access to the Department's gym and general office area. He still got along with most of the guys. Mike could go pretty much everywhere but the exhibit locker. Because of a bad audit a year ago, the Department insured that only one Rolicking manager had access to exhibits at any one time. This was the company line. Mike also knew that, no matter what, Earl could always get in the locker. The corporate issue was now one of creating the illusion of greater control by painting a tainted picture of absolute control. Like most cops, Earl would only work in the exhibit locker if absolutely required. Exhibit management was not something to fight over. Mike's computer privileges were also deemed off limits. The tekkies, God love them; had an automatic fail-safe that kicked in with the suspension notice.

He knew about the old trapper's Enfield for years. It was really no big deal. He was a harmless happy drunk most times. He went willingly to the tank. Their business relationship had evolved very slowly. Ernie would deliver the odd street package while the sergeant would treat him that much better in cells. In the trapper's mind he was simply being sent on another Ranger mission. Just like Vegas, the cops had all the latitude in the world to comp any street client to a suite. Sometimes, he would just give Ernie an envelope and nothing would be said. There really was no need. It was money to belong in the street. Mike needed Ernie tuned into business. The old trapper always made sure that he cleared it with him before going back to Wandering Lake. It was like finding the nose on your face—he was always beside the Inn. He knew he did the right thing to give the trapper a ride to cells that night. That following morning when he was released from the tank, they met. The map that could not be lost was sketched. It was only supposed to be for a day or two.

Mike thought about the product in the exhibit locker that needed to be moved. It was easy when he was the exhibit custodian. He went into the locker six times a day moving exhibits in and out. Each exhibit movement was "in theory" painstakingly tracked in the system. It was the nature of his duties that he moved seized items into the locker and court required items out. Ron was a good kid. It really was too bad that his service weapon was now dressed with such a sordid past.

Ron would never suspect. There would never be a comparison. He was openly shopping for another job in the big city. The gun would simply be turned back into the RCP when he left. Sidearms that are returned to the RCP are simply secured in the exhibit locker. A necessary waiting place until their time is once more due. Another new cop will eventually arrive and they could be issued a new weapon or simply, one of the spare 9 mm's.

At this point, there was a noticeable abundance of chance. He still had the spare 9 mm and there was no way to get back in the locker—not quite yet. There were just too many dead ends right now. It was a failing in plot execution that pissed the sergeant off. He had always admired bad guys that pulled off a good sting while openly admonishing those that fucked things up. The old cop now found himself in the latter category. Sergeant Funk turned away from the window while considering, there were bad guys and gangsters—bad guys know the limits.

Chapter 20
The Trail

Kate, Earl and Mushy looked around the entrance of the hotel. The distant bar could be seen to the extreme south side of the small restaurant. Behind the counter was the small confectionary comprised of chocolate bars, gum, peanuts, chips and cigarettes. There was also the usual assortment of key chains, maps and tourist brochures. Surprisingly, there was a map of Hill Mountain which consisted of four intersecting lines. It displayed the main road into town with the bridge. This was known by the locals as Betla's Creek. The creek flowed south to north much like the Red River. It emptied into Shallow Lake on the East side. It was very well known because of the excellent fishing in June at the Creek's mouth.

Earl turned to Kate, "Do you know this creek very well?"

Kate licked the ketchup seasoning from her fingers and looked wide eyed at Earl. She wasn't sure herself if his questions formed the basis of cathartic insight or the initiation of a cheap one liner. Kate replied, "I know nothing of this creek, river or most things outside of Rolicking. What's the point? Are you talking about the water under the bridge … into town? The one that the street guy walked by … you know."

Earl took an unusually long time to respond. He just kept looking at the map. He turned to his partner, "No one in Hill Mountain had seen McIvor for a day. His only set of wheels was still in town. Did he hitch a ride with one hand? Fuck, I can't find my truck keys with two hands! How would that play out? Even if he could, would he drive with one hand? Detective tell me, if you were going to off someone in Hill Mountain where would you do it?"

Kate replied immediately, "Well it would have to be away unless it was a knife and you didn't care. A bullet shot would be heard for half a mile." Kate looked at the old staff; she had seen that same look many times before. It was the combination of an intense glare accompanied with the painful jolt of a sudden burn.

Earl looked out the door of the hotel which led into the darkness. Through the hotel window he could see the Confinement Team standing around, waiting. The white encased scientists were still hard at work, hunched over in the distance. Several of the Team members were in the process of assisting Ident with the installation of a tarp over the scene. If it got much colder they would have to get the big kerosene heaters into the tent. Earl wished he was closer to "ear ball" the chatter. Several members of the Confinement Team, obviously under the direction of Ident, were now changing into the much more "refined" bunny suits. If you looked closely at the scientist's rule book, commando apparel was heavily testosterone contaminated and simply never to be worn inside a crime scene.

Mushy walked into the hotel leaving Licit in the truck. He rubbed his eyes while flipping back his RCP issued ball cap. He too perused the McTavish cuisine samplings and bucked tradition by purchasing a cola and cheezies. Mushy looked down at the cheezies and commented, "Licit really likes these." He gave the owner the requested $6.25 for the items. He said, "Fucking highway—fucking robbery." He then turned to McTavish and asked him for a receipt. Mushy grabbed the goodies and commented to Earl and Kate, "If we are going to track we might as well do it right now. After the rain the scent will be useless."

Earl thought to himself that Mushy had a valid point. They might as well send the dog back to Rolicking if the rain came. The scientists could work under the tarp but the dog needed a decent scent. Decent scents did not tend to stick around forever. By virtue of physics, the night dew was pretty much a track killer. Earl longed to keep Mushy around even it was simply for the comedic value. Like Kate, there was always comfort in having cops around that could maintain perspective. Mushy and his stir stick assault on the boss would forever live as a local country ballad.

Earl did not say a word to Kate or Mushy. He stepped away from the counter. He picked up his portable radio which sat simply in the inside pocket of his sports jacket. He radioed Harold, "Superintendent Thompson ... Jeans"

Harold replied immediately, "Go ahead ... 20?" Twenty simply meant a cop's way of asking, "Where the hell are you?" Sometimes the transmitter of the message truly cared. Most times it was just to make sure that a subordinate was not fucking around. Harold had tacked the code at the end of the sentence thereby inferring an immediate reply.

Earl keyed the radio and stated simply, "Lobby."

The District boss further clarified, "Come to where I'm at…"

Earl stared at Kate and Mushy while rolling his eyes, "Where exactly would your *at* be…?"

Harold clarified, "Up the stairs we're checked in, Room 14."

It was Mushy's turn to gawk in amusement at the group. He shrugged as the trio resolved themselves to the unusually steep climb up the old stairs. As if conjured up by a movie stunt coordinator, the creaking of the stairs was totally appropriate given the rustic setting. The ambiance was completed with the tail end finish of Van Morrison's "G.L.O.R.I.A." There was no satellite radio in the hotel. The juke box clicked, grabbed and then dropped another vinyl disc. This tune was by Abba, "Dancing Queen."

Only because of his profound stamina, Mushy was the first to reach the pinnacle of the steps. There was a bank of four rooms as expected. There was one dirty window at the end of the hall which faced the crime scene. The old gold lettering on the doors identified all four rooms as 11, 12, 13 and 14. It could have easily been rooms 1, 2, 3 and 4 but McTavish had learned early in the hotelier game to create an enhanced sense of grandeur. Even with the obvious four rooms, many Americans still asked for something on the lower level.

Earl stared at Room 14 and cynically commented, "Yep, he just had to have a corner suite with two fucking windows." Earl banged on the door but he didn't wait for a response. He walked in with the group behind him. Sergeant Bernie was seated at a ridiculously small table beside Harold.

Harold commented, "P.B. came by, he has nothing and I doubt very much that he will tonight. We have rented all the rooms available which are 13 and 14. P.B. will be bunking in 13 with the sergeant."

Earl knew it was supposed to be one of those standoff social situations. In reality, it was much more of an opportunity to escape. The superintendent was astute enough to realize that no sleeping arrangements had been considered for the others.

Earl piped up, "Good stuff, have a nice night. We'll go to my cabin on Shallow Lake. Here these are for you." He reached inside his sports jacket and tossed the boss the gingerbread men. The now grease soaked paper bag bounced off the small table. One of the gingerbread men bounced and broke at the waist. Earl could not have planned it any better. The leg less gingerbread man covered in red and yellow icing peered up, ever so friendly, with his frosted Manitoba smile. After the cookies were tossed, Earl did not wait for a reply. He turned an about face with Kate. Mushy followed closely to the rear. There wasn't any further small talk. On the descent downstairs, Kate felt around the bottom of her bag for some residual ketchup flavored crumbs—nada.

Kate sadly reflected, "I would have killed for a gingerbread man. When the hell did you put them in your pocket?"

Earl replied, "When I got out the signs. I hated to waste them on the old man but sometimes you just have to seize the moment at the greater expense of personal sacrifice." The old staff reached inside his jacket and switched off the police radio. At the bottom of the stairs he stopped at the front counter and bought a "24" of beer." In the big picture, the cost of the beer was much better value than soda and chips! The restaurant was now officially closed. The black and white sign hung diagonally on the door window. The plastic clock hands indicated a very low tech reopening time of 7:00 A.M. The group walked down the street and on to their respective police vehicles.

Earl turned to Mushy and asked, "Do you have time for a quick track?" Mushy and Kate turned their heads in utter disbelief. It was now well after 10:00 P.M. The rain had not started but the wind was picking up. Prompted by the enquiring look on their faces, Earl continued, "....not far just under the bridge."

Mushy just shrugged. He climbed into his truck, lowered the driver's window and loudly shouted into the night, "Hey you bought the 24 your call."

The Confinement Team members had now split up. Half the Team was sleeping on the bus while the others loosely guarded the Co-op. On the way over to the bridge Kate and Earl did not talk. Kate silently wondered about the bridge. Things always seemed to happen under any bridge. To the dope dealer, or most criminals, under the bridge was a safe place. Under the bridge was after all, the meeting place for pay offs, adolescent sex, fishing, drug injections, wiener roasts, graffiti painting and especially beer sampling. For everyone else, typically residing over the bridge, under the bridge implied deception.

* * * *

P.B. climbed up the stairs with his black notebook in hand. He had already clarified the bunking arrangements with Sergeant Bernie. It was no big deal in the big scheme of things. Nothing much was going on in town. In any event, it was too late for normal folks to answer their doors. In all likelihood, if something ever happened at the Co-op after dark, it would never have been noticed. There was zero possibility in the big picture that anyone saw a violent confrontation. P.B. found himself in front of "Room 14." He quietly tapped on the door. Harold opened it a crack. The chain was clearly in place. P.B. could only see the whites of Harold's left eye through the door opening. The District boss unhooked the chain. It swung and bounced loudly off the door jamb. The superintendent reached out quickly to contain the rebounding racket. Reaching down to the interior knob, Harold repositioned the old bilingual cardboard sign to the exterior knob. The sign swung several times like a guillotine blade. It read, "Do Not Disturb—Ne me moleste pas."

P.B. walked into the confines of the corner suite and closed the door. The suite was dreary, uninviting and bleak by even 70's standards. There was only one light which was housed in a metallic gold floor lamp fixture. The light had no glass or shroud. It simply consisted of a floor lamp stem and bulb. The bulb flickered as if already knowing that its days were numbered. P.B's immediate attention was drawn to the length of rebar resting on the table. The superintendent was draped in a shear purple smoking jacket. The jacket had two deep side pockets and a karate type black sash tie as a closure. The material had a satin like sheen. It looked horribly out of place given the seedy flavor of the environment. The District emblem in bright blue and yellow was embroidered on the jacket. The only thing Harold lacked was the seemingly obligatory ascot.

There was no ice, no bucket and certainly no champagne. On the table were several diet colas positioned smartly beside the rebar. The rebar was protected in a velvet lined jewelers case. It was positioned in the geographic center of the round table. Much like a pyramid, the rebar was believed to emit energy. There were strangely no pips, formalities or pretense. If only Dr. Shelby knew how one length of rod could change a man forever.

* * * *

The Crown Vic pulled over to the town side of the bridge. Earl reached into his kit bag and pulled out the dented "Maglite." Kate reached into the console and pulled out a push button flashlight that was affixed to a headband. Mushy exited the truck and instructed Licit to track. Kate and Earl followed from a distance making sure not to confuse the dog. Mushy hurled doggie encouragements at Licit. The dog was clearly energized and happy to be finally working. The bank along the creek was noticeably muddy. The creek had receded over the summer and the mud gave up its previously watery past. Along the bed were the expected beer cans, chip bags and condoms. Earl noticed the Alliance "ALL" painted on the side of the bridge. He turned to Kate, "Did you know that this was Alliance's hood?"

Kate replied, "No I didn't ... it just never occurred to me that Alliance would be active in a small town. There is no drug trade to speak of and there are no factions. How would we have known?"

The team continued to walk under the bridge from the north then a zig zag to the south side. The dog ran and turned, often times spinning in circles. His head pecks left the impression of conflicting scents. To state there were some tracks would be to under state the obvious. The dog continued to dart in and out of scents while continually sniffing to the ground. Licit's muzzle did not come up for air. His head remained fixed to the target.

The dog tracked south past the bridge and into a wooded area. Strangely enough, right in the middle of a clearing was an old bordello type, floral trimmed, puke gold sofa and matching arm chair. The arm chair was right out of a 70's sitcom. It looked completely out of place in a mystery. There was really no discerning if the dog was onto a trail that "mattered" or simply mesmerized by a more interesting stink. There were the remains of a camp fire that was long since cold. The ash sat inside a small circle of gray river rock. Strewn around was a potpourri of discarded beer and hair spray cans.

Earl stooped down on one knee. He closely examined a yellow surveying ribbon fastened to a tree branch. These ribbons were all over the North. They were mostly left by the highway marking levels that had been surveyed. Clearly, the bordello did not appear to be salvageable in a television makeover. The wind continued to pick up and the slim poplar and birch trees creaked objections in the night. The dog continued past the rustic living room set and further back into the dense bush. The trio walked through the bush carefully catching swinging branches in order to best avoid getting smashed in the face. The rain coupled with the night air and stomping only served to further rile up the mosquitoes. There was no escaping their constant burrowing into any available skin.

Kate was fed up with the current situation. She flung her arms constantly battling the pests. The detective was dressed for the city and not a walk in the woods. It was one thing for Earl in a sports jacket but quite the opposite in semi-designer apparel. The Rolicking City definition of a "semi-designer pant" was an article of clothing that could easily be purchased at the hardware store. The garment was functional for an office environment yet horribly out of context for a cold trek in the woods.

Mushy turned to his two partners and commented, "There is still a scent but we cannot go any further tonight. We simply can't see enough. It's too damn dangerous for the dog. If Licit took off right now, there could easily be two crime scenes!"

Earl reflected for a moment then posed the question, "How can you tell if there is a scent worth following tomorrow or just a fucking stink from other bush clans?"

Mushy called Licit, the dog looked up and sat down at his master's left leg. His eyes gave away his desire to continue on. Mushy clarified his position, "I know we're getting rain, we may never have a trail. A scent is simply a stink that could matter. To answer your question, there is no way to really tell the difference between trails—the hottest one gets the grease. Tell you what, walk up the hill and Licit will be happy to demonstrate for you how the dog can track a stink. Of course, please do not take my remark out of context. I certainly mean no disrespect to the keeper of the beer."

Earl turned to Kate, "Throw me the keys. I'll drive to the cabin. Mushy you follow. Hope things won't be too cold." From the wooded area Earl could see the roof lights of the idling Team bus. The space helmeted space creatures held tightly onto to their lasers in the night. The film set was still ablaze. The bunny suits reflected their shape as distant shadows through the tarp. The trackers had circled around from the creek and were now positioned to the extreme outskirts of Hill Mountain. Earl had been there before. The trail was not that far from the cabin. The rain was now coming down heavy from the west; it pelted their faces.

Kate was noticeably unhappy with her current situation. A weak and understated, "For fucks sakes…." was wearily tossed out by the detective. The gents said nothing and silently acquiesced to Kate's sentiments. If the old staff wasn't so tired, he would have been right on Kate for wanting to quit. It simply wasn't the time to chuck shit. In the movies there never seems to be a logistically impossible crime scene—Northern Manitoba has nothing but….

Chapter 21
Make No Judgment

Earl sat in the driver's seat of the Crown Vic while Kate relaxed in the passenger seat. His hands held the steering wheel very loosely while he focused on the dismal drive. The rain had greatly compounded the overall issue of visibility.

Earl turned to Kate in the dark, "I'm awake all of a sudden. I was okay but once we bought the beer … it must be the liquor anxiety. It would have been better if there was some real booze but the only outlet outside of Rolicking was in the Co-op. Gotta tell you, I considered breaking into the store but some viper would probably snipe my ass."

Kate kept her eyes focused on the heaving road. There could always be a something sitting on a roadway. Kate said, "Those vipers would knock up an extra round of points if they picked off your old butt. If you screwed with the Co-op, Harold would probably hang the whole caper on you. You didn't do it did you?"

Earl laughed, "Did what, cut off a hand or put a bullet in 9 Ball's head?"

Kate, "That would be 8 Ball's head—the 9 ball is yellow."

The old staff thought for a moment and dug deep into his right pocket. It was reflex more than anything. He grabbed the pill bottle—no reassuring rattle, empty. He commented, "I don't know if I'll be able to sleep, just too much going on. I guess a guy should give it a go. I also have to break the news to you that the water lines are out so you'll have to use the outhouse."

There was a time when Kate would have baulked at outdoor plumbing but not tonight. She really didn't care as long as the damn door closed and she had some semblance of privacy.

Earl said, "The cabin is just down to the right, the first road. I'm only "2 K" from town. It didn't always seem so damn close but a lot of the bush has grown over. Most of the trails between the cabin and the town intertwine and end up on the south side of town. There is pretty good game in the bush, even close by. Did I tell you that I have my moose picked out. He's a pretty big bull. I've been watching him damn close since the spring. Nice rack too … but one side is a little bashed up from years of battle induced abuse. Certainly, nothing I could pass up. Bet you'd never figure, that a guy that can't even thumb fuck a cell phone, would be such a swell outdoorsman! Wait till I show you my toy."

The Crown Vic found its way slowly down "Road 1" by the billboard and around the big curve. Cabins were dotted along the shoreline. The lake could only be seen in brief patches of open space that flashed between cabins. The rain, fog and a hidden moon prevented any further sense of geographic orientation. Earl pulled the car past the driveway and then swung the gear shift into reverse. Kate cranked her head around but she had no immediate sense of a defined driveway. The only noise was the constant creaking of the crickets and the hum of the mosquitoes in the trees. Kate could not put her finger on the noise but it sounded as if a hydro transformer was buzzing in the tree tops, it was now 11:20 P.M. Earl exited the Crown Vic. He couldn't wait to open up the outhouse. He walked up to a tree by the driveway, unzipped his pants and had a pee. Kate still in the car, shrugged it off thinking, life should be so easy!

Mushy's truck drove slightly past the driveway. As if decreed on males worldwide, he simply backed quickly and effortlessly into the driveway. Kate watched on and shook her head. There was something in the male DNA that better tolerated reverse action. Both vehicles were now almost blocking the driveway to the Cabin.

* * * *

Ernie glanced out the kitchen window. He wondered if the police had finally arrived. There was nothing in the plan for tonight. Maybe it was him, had he fallen asleep in the dark? There was really no way to account for time other than the fire. He hadn't thrown more wood in the stove. It had to be the same night. Something must have changed or gone wrong. The meet was not supposed to be until the next day, right? His mind blazoned with thoughts and possibilities. Should he run? If he ran, what was he running from…? His ears made out voices. There were several; it made no sense. The old trapper reached for the large backpack in the dark. His body crawled along the cold vinyl floor of the kitchen. He raised himself slowly over the old stove while eyeballing the oncoming shadows through the kitchen window. There was no glass in the woodstove. The only light afforded was projected through the spots of fire that bounced through the small cracks on the iron cooking grate. It cast pockets of airborne light that ricocheted off the walls and ceiling. The old trapper instinctively loaded a clip into the Enfield. For the first time in his life—the click of the magazine disturbed him.

Ernie waited patiently while still leaning over the top of the old stove. He could see the silhouette of the vehicles. He heard nothing but hard rain. There was the back door that he had used to check out the property. They could come in that way. Maybe there was a trap door in the floor. Ernie gazed around the cabin trying to absorb a greater sense of tactical options. The old trapper's hands clutched the Enfield with a very uncustomary steel grip. His rib was in the most awkward position possible. Ernie tried to muffle an involuntary cough.

* * * *

Earl zipped up and noticed the yellow ribbon while smelling smoke in the air. The smell could often be misleading in the rain. He looked above the roofline and onto the chimney. There was no mistaking the origination of the fire. Earl was first in line to the deck. Kate second and Mushy pulled up the rear. Licit started to jump and bark in the truck. The bumper vibrated, rebounding up and down. The only illumination on the deck was a faint light cast from the distant outhouse.

Earl whispered while placing a hand on Kate's shoulder, "Stay down." He pushed her forcefully to the left side of the main door and away from the kitchen window. Kate stumbled back over a small stack of firewood but quickly regained her composure.

Earl said while drawing his service weapon, "I think we have company. There is condensation inside the windows and there is smoke. It feels damn ugly." Mushy was now beside his two partners forcing himself flat against the wall. In the hope of a better vantage point, he slowly made his way around to the southernmost side of the cabin.

Earl said, "God damn it … not even one beer! I just never thought someone would be in here. No vehicle, it looked the same as usual. Fuck sakes."

Kate replied, "Looked the same as usual … just fucking great! I'm here with my gun out wearing my god damned cocktail shoes—and you thought it looked liked usual." The old staff peered laterally across the door to catch a glimpse of something. Kate continued, "You look like a god damned turtle. Can you do that again with your neck? Maybe they fucked off and left. The cabin could be empty."

Earl said, "I heard something. You can't creep quietly around the cabin. Feet shuffling always sound like a pair of heavy old tits rubbing on barn boards."

* * * *

Kate leaned over to Earl's left ear, "I was going to guard this with my life but you have a fucking big hair growing out of your ear. I can't stand the thing. I will yank it first chance I get. Just in case this turns out bad—can you please take care of your hygiene."

Earl said, "You are such a close friend. I can't tell you how much of a help you've been. I won't die in front of my own cabin. I'd never live it down."

Kate took a moment to absorb the sentiment. It was one of those "Earl'isms" that was either very deep or damn shallow. Sometimes you can't really tell if you're already in the water. Kate leaned towards the dangling follicle, "We have to do something. I'm wet and I'm getting a Charlie horse from this crouch. You're the closest to the door. Just lean over and open it up a little so we can see in. I got your hairy back. You got squat to worry about." At the corner of the south side of the cabin, Earl could see Mushy waiving his fingers, almost like he was finger spelling for the deaf.

Earl leaned over to Kate and said, "Mush thinks I know that commando hand signal shit. Honest to fuck, these guys drive me nuts. Can you go over and talk to him. Just tell him the dog would come in handy. If we can open the door … we can let Licit in there. Of course, he's going to have to get him out of the truck."

Kate crept on all fours swearing under her breath. She was caught between an Earl and a hard place. She liked the idea. Why not fire in the dog? Most times the dog or master was laid up when you really needed them. Holy fuck, we have the dog and master! Holy shit, she found it strange to finally realize that they had a valued police option at their disposal. Kate looked down at her pants and mumbled under her breath, "District's going to get a receipt for these Rolik-Mart numbers."

Mushy saw Kate's shadow creeping along the edge of the cabin wall. He came around the south side to meet her half way. Mushy crouched over and leaned his ass back on one leg. Kate remained on all fours. In her mind it was just simpler. Like a steel ball in pin ball machine, the detective had this tainted vision that she would be rebounding information all night. Mushy leaned down to Kate, "I'm going to go and get the dog. I don't particularly give a shit what Earl told you."

Kate looked up at Mushy, like a puppy at his master. She batted her eyes ever so slightly. Her neck was turned upwards in a noticeably forced and awkward position. She clarified, "Earl wants you to climb up on the roof and rappel down the other side of the cabin. Then swing yourself into the cabin through the living room window."

Mushy, "I'm getting the dog."

Kate, "You're going to rappel with the dog—fucking bonus!"

Mushy leaned over and went back to his truck the long way around scampering in and out through the puny Manitoba trees. The rain remained constant and the trio were now thoroughly soaked. Kate held back a shiver which made her far too conscious of her current discomfort. She turned an abrupt 180 degrees and scurried back on all fours to Earl.

* * * *

Ernie held fast. He could hear a truck door slam in the distance and then barking. It made no sense. If it was Alliance why would they have a dog? Maybe someone was just letting out another dog for a pee? Maybe it was just another dog that had happened by? He slid slowly back down from his perch on the stove. It was more out of a greater sense of tactical repositioning than imminent fear. He knew he could not outrun a dog in the dark. The back door exit was no longer an option. He would now have to wait. The rainy night presented no other recourse.

Ernie could now hear other voices in the distance. They seemed to be everywhere. The dog's growling amplified off the front door. The snarl permeated the air like the animal was already in the kitchen. Ernie braced his back against the lower kitchen cabinets. His legs were stretched out in front. The Enfield hovered at waist level and was pointed towards the front door. He found himself somewhat sheltered by the confines of the kitchen table. The trapper did not have the rifle sighted. It remained pointed from the hip while it swung laterally in the air. Ernie's breathing was strained beneath his sore chest and overly fatigued body. His heart beat audibly in his head as it pounded far beneath the drab canvas jacket.

* * * *

Mushy had now repositioned himself at the front door with Licit held tightly on leash. Earl watched the dog's mouth carefully. He reached out within inches of the teeth. He gently turned the knob clockwise—it was unlocked.

Mushy whispered, "It's okay they'll be right behind us."

Earl heard, "It's okay…." The door knob was now almost fully rotated to the open position. Kate was now up and hovered precariously over Earl's left side. The old staff ever so slowly turned the remainder of free play in the knob. Mushy stared at both the door and the kitchen window. Unleashing the dog, Mushy held onto Licit tightly by the collar. The dog was now up high. His full weight rested on his two rear legs. He foamed wildly at the mouth while spit splashed at the door.

Earl's attention was refocused to the intermittent lights that drifted at various heights around the perimeter. There were more flickering light beams in the bush. It looked out of place to see the lights projecting high and low among the poplar and spruce. The old staff wiped the rain from his eyes. He listened to the sounds of boots crushing on distant dead fall.

There was a very small margin of dry protection offered by the eaves of the cabin. Like a game of horse and rider, Kate was now almost on top of Earl's back. The trio and dog were now more like one bulky mass than separate people. Earl moved remarkably fast. Simultaneously, he released the knob while kicking the door open.

Mushy hollered, "Licit get em' and released the dog's collar." The old staff fell back into Kate as he immediately sprung himself back from Licit's oncoming path.

Mushy's portable echoed out, "Team Leader … position."

* * * *

Ernie noticed a flicker of light flash as the front door swung open. Illuminated rain pounded in and flooded the interior of the cabin. The front door struck hard and bounced violently off the interior wall. The injured trapper felt wet with the sudden involuntary release of fear. He aimed the Enfield towards the door and pulled the trigger. The shot was deafening within the confines of tight space. Licit gnarled and lunged at the old trapper biting hard into the calf of his extended left leg. Mushy was the first one through the door after the dog. Sidearms were pointed in the general direction of the dark mass huddled beside the kitchen cabinets.

Ernie cried out in the dark, "Help me. Help me!"

In the midst of the attack, the old trapper heard voices from the back of the cabin, "Rolicking Police."

Ernie flailed his leg in agony while Licit continued to gnaw harder into his leg. The dog shook his head relentlessly as he sunk his teeth deeper and deeper. Ernie instinctively lifted the canvas jacket to protect his head. He hung onto to the Enfield and pulled the bolt back. The dark shadows of the "camo dressed" figures stood at the rear door. Several shots rang out in Ernie's direction and his torso slumped slowly to the floor.

* * * *

Mushy ran towards Licit commanding, "Out, Licit, out!" The dog master pulled back forcibly on the collar while clipping the leash.

There was now silence in the cabin. Earl gazed at the camo garbed invaders and the broken rear door. Earl and Kate stared at Ron Fleury who was among the camo pack with his 9 mm drawn. Dressed in a T-shirt and blue jeans, he looked horribly foreign against the darker backdrop of the Team. The .303 round and deemed "friendly fire" had missed the dog. Licit continued to bark at the stationary mass that remained motionless beneath the blood soaked clothes.

Mushy ran at Fleury and several other Team members, "You fuckers, for taking a god damn shot anywhere near my dog. That's not my wife. That's my fucking dog!" Mushy crossed the cabin floor and grabbed Ron. Several Confinement members jumped in between.

Earl reached down to the floor and pushed away the jacket to reveal the trapper's face, "I know this guy—he's a local." The staff looked up, "Kate you okay?"

Kate looked on at the crumpled object. Her head wrapped flashlight beam now projected squarely on the trapper's face. Earl stood up and turned on the main cabin lights. He commented, "This is going to do squat for resale value. You guys know that."

His comment was directed at no one in particular. It was simply stated out of a greater obligation to mitigate tension. The Confinement Team members looked on. There was no greater need to comment further.

Phillip Rothersay hollered, "Clear the cabin." With that command, Confinement broke up and searched the remainder of the building. Beams of helmeted lights bounced throughout the bedroom areas while Constable Fleury remained motionless.

Ron Fleury stared at the canvassed covered mass. His eyes fixated on Ernie's face. Ron still held onto his service weapon. He mechanically and methodically dropped the clip then cleared the chambered round. The bullet flew several feet and then bounced on the wooden floor. He turned to Earl while locking open the action and offered up the weapon, handle first to Earl. There was no doubt in the Rookie's mind that one of his rounds had hit the intended target.

Ron moved closer to Earl while continuing to look down. In a quiet and respectful voice, he asked, "May I hold my Father?"

Earl took the extended weapon with his left hand while draping his right hand over the young cop. Earl quietly asked him, "Are you sure?"

Ron replied, "Yes, I would know him anywhere."

Earl walked over with Ron and reached down to lift the jacket over Ernie's face. He looked at the old rifle still cradled in the trapper's cold hands. It was one of the hardest moments in the staff's life. He looked back up to Ron and told him, "You can look but please do not touch your dad. I know it's asking the impossible but please do your best." Ron noticeably shivered and rubbed his arms. Earl drew him closer towards the trapper while regulating his posture. He held the rookie's 9 mm, action open, by his left leg.

Earl said, "All this time, you never told anyone. You saw him when you were guarding. You must have arrested him yourself when his was drunk, everyone did."

Ron replied, "I kept it quiet ... I was too embarrassed."

Kate overhead pieces of the conversation and reached up to kill her headlight beam. She crouched beside Earl and shivered from the combination of cold, wet and death in the air. The old staff reached around and removed his wet sports jacket. He then draped it over Kate's shoulders.

Earl instructed Kate, "You have to get out of the wet clothes. There are some dry ones in Judy's set of drawers." The cabin wasn't warm but it was dry and more comfortable than the alternative.

Mushy bent over and pet Licit, "Good dog, good dog." It wasn't an accolade in response to the death of the old man. It was rather, praise as Licit had performed exactly as he must.

Earl still crouched, rose up to his feet and looked at Mushy. "How did the ninja's get here?"

Mushy replied, "I called them from the truck."

Earl, "Swell and Ron just came by...?"

Mushy responded, still angry while looking at Ron, "I have no fucking idea how the hell he got here!"

Ron clarified, "I was on the road. I ... was driving a car for Mike ... just going to the city. I had the portable on. I heard Mushy's call for Confinement—I was ten minutes away." The young cop remained attentive and seemingly glued to the motionless mass.

Mushy shrugged off the explanation while Earl continued a cursory examination of the dead trapper. Mushy leashed Licit and left the cabin. There were numerous additional trucks and one RX-7 parked diagonally in the driveway. There were other vehicles strewn on the shoulder of the main gravel road.

Earl looked over the old yet familiar canvas jacket and noticed several points of entry. At least one .308 large caliber entry and another that looked like a possible 9 mm. The old staff had been in these situations before he would have to call the boss. There would be process and necessary follow up.

Earl checked on Kate in the back bedroom. The door was only slightly ajar. She looked strange in Judy's old blue sweats with the white side stripe. It was more like she was off to a track meet then a detective at a crime scene. Earl walked closer to Kate and said, "Take a look at the trapper's hand. It looks like a map. There is writing on the palm and a number. I don't understand why the hell he was here. I'm pretty sure he didn't happen to jot down a number and then die in a shoot out. Ernie was just in town the other night. I saw him staggering around the streets. I'm pretty sure he ended up in cells."

* * * *

Mushy walked his dog slowly while weaving in and out among the trees that bordered the driveway. The dog took his time dragging out an extended pee. The presumed mission was to squarely hit each and every tire. In Licit's mind, the higher the hit—the tougher the dog. Mushy reached into his side pocket and gave Licit a treat. The rain had now slowed down to a dull sprinkling. Mushy wiped his wet forehead and then leaned down to pet the dog's thick coat. In mid pee, the dog stopped at the rear of the RX-7 and "indicated." The indication was consistent with a suspicious "stink" from the back of the car. Licit's nose was planted firmly against the right wheel well. The car was low to the ground. The dog's nose nuzzled the sleek metal body. He whimpered and spun once then barked at the car. Mushy looked through the rear of the hatchback window. He half expected to see a body. The dog master opened the passenger door and an envelope tumbled to the soaked ground.

Epilogue

The day after the trapper's death an extensive search was conducted by Mushy and the Confinement Team. They tracked the wooded area between the cabin and the Co-op and found the partially animal eaten body of Jason McIvor. The legs, arms and head had been chewed off and dragged into the brush. At Earl's request, an examination of the trapper's Enfield was made with the bullet that killed McIvor. The old Enfield was conclusively determined to be the same weapon used to kill McIvor.

The search of the Co-op and seizure of the hand provided no further evidence as to its rightful owner. The ring on the finger was consistent with insignia from a rival gang that was attempting to step on Alliance's action. Fingerprints were run and DNA typing would be retained for future analysis. No other suspicious limbs were found in the Co-op.

There was a post mortem in Winnipeg conducted two days later. One 9 mm slug was removed from the trapper consistent with a hollow point police issued bullet. There was one other point of entry presumed to be the result of a .308 Confinement Team hit. The rifle slug had exited the body and was eventually located under the cabin floor.

* * * *

Earl knocked on Mike Funk's door it was now 11:00 A.M. and Ashley answered. Earl did not give her a chance to speak and simply enquired, "Is your dad here? It is urgent." Mike Funk walked down the stairs while knotting his bath robe sash.

He asked the old staff, "Is everything okay ... did something happen to the car?"

Earl spoke to Ashley calmly, "Your dad and I will have to go to the office."

A comparison of the 9 mm slug found at the 8 Ball and Ernie Moose shootings confirmed that they were likely fired from the same weapon. Oddly, there was no consistency with the impression marks left by the firing pin. The tip of the hollow point round seized in the 8 Ball killing was mushroomed as expected. However, it still retained sufficient lands and grooves for ballistic comparison.

* * * *

Earl and Kate walked into Raven's and ordered two coffees. One normal black and one subtly jazzed up. They took a seat beside the plants while Earl immediately swatted one big leaf out of the way.

The staff said, "These fucking plants—why don't they trash them? I'll have to call Health. Plastic in a coffee can't be a good thing."

Kate looked at Earl and laughed. She thought how dull life would be if he ever left. It never made perfect sense to her. Most of it did but there were still some unanswered questions. Kate asked, "You never did tell me why Mike admitted the killings?"

Earl replied, "Sure I did, you just don't remember. I meant to show you."

Kate sat up and drank her coffee while staring intently at Earl. She tried to remember something that could matter. Kate commented, "You're speaking in tongues again. Okay I'm old too … I forget."

Earl reached into the zippered nylon brief case and pulled out a small GPS looking device. It was grey and black with a small tinted screen. Kate looked at it somewhat perplexed. Earl said, "You remember … at the cabin, when I was going to show you my toy. This is my "Mooz-Kam 200.""

Kate, "Your what…?"

Earl clarified, "That big bull, there are cameras all around the bush. They send signals to the receiver in the cabin. There must be half a dozen cameras out there. I often forget where they are so I use yellow ribbons as markers. Good thing they can't be seen or sure as shit they would get ripped off! I didn't get a camera shot of Mike actually killing McIvor. I did get a picture of him walking by a camera holding the Enfield. To be honest, beats me if we could ever say conclusively if it was the Enfield. Once Mike knew about the cameras and Fleury shooting his poor dad … he just dumped his load. I really didn't need the picture anyway—that was leverage. Ballistics did the rest. Kind of ironic that the weapon he used to set up the trapper actually solved the file."

Kate commented, "How the hell did Funk get the rifle?"

Earl lowered his glasses to the end of his nose and replied, "Check the cell block system. Funk always came in by the cell block door to use the gym. He already had the Enfield then he went out to Hill Mountain and killed McIvor. He had all night until Ernie was released. Of course, Funk couldn't control everything. He had no way of knowing that Fleury would get involved. Ron's a good kid he'll make it through this. I guess Funk must have been doing this for years. Earl looked down while lowering his voice; you remember—he wasn't always like this. "

Kate looked away. Her mental gears were obviously grinding hard to catch up. She asked, "He had the Enfield but I don't …."

Earl picked up in midstream and finished, "Don't blame yourself, this one's a little tricky. He kept Ernie's backpack when he dropped him off at cells. Ernie was likely too juiced to notice. I verified with the prisoner booking sheet. No backpack is mentioned. Remarkable coincidence, the same night McIvor ends up dead, Ernie was in cells."

Kate's eyes gave up her confusion. She asked, "I still don't get how Funk worked the backpack return. He picked up the trapper in his truck?"

Earl clarified, "Funk had no choice on the ride to cells. It was either the ride to cells and keep the backpack, or wait until Ernie was in cells. If he waited, he would have had to snatch the Enfield from the backpack—tricky shit indeed. It was much easier to simply return the entire backpack. Funk then returned to Rolicking to work out like he always did at 5:00 A.M. We don't have airport security yet so the camera doesn't tell us the color of Funk's boxers or what's inside his gym bag. Mike was at the gym long before release time. That's when he made the drop. The guard didn't account for everything when Ernie was released. They never do. The trapper signed the prisoner sheet, went into the garage, picked up the backpack and left through the garage. In Ernie's mind, it was pretty much like any other morning exiting the cell block. I always wondered why Mike had such a damn big bag. Gym bag, you know…. I guess once in awhile he dropped off an Enfield. Other times … he moved out guns and coke. When you think about it, there is no safer place to stash dope than a cop shop."

Kate asked, "So why did he bother to return the Enfield? He could have just kept it."

Earl replied, "He had to return the Enfield. Sober, Ernie would have freaked in cells if the backpack was missing. The gun also had to be there or necessarily someone else murdered McIvor. Remember, the plan was to finger the old trapper. Easy enough to do once Funk put Ernie, McIvor and the Enfield at my fucking cabin. Do you know what .308 rounds do to kitchen cabinets? Perhaps you can tell—I'm a little pissed off."

* * * *

157

Val peered in her cooler and wondered when the plant that was ordered from Winnipeg would be picked up? It was an unusually large rubber plant contained in a massive black pot. It had sat there for a more than a week now. It had to go. She took it out of the cooler and jammed a white plastic, "For Sale" sign in the plant's soil.

At the same time, a package remained dormant at the Hill Mountain Co-op. It had not been claimed by the Rolicking City business recipient, "Andi's Restoration." It was very odd that he had not come by fishing this week. If the package wasn't picked up soon, it would have to be returned.

* * * *

Several weeks had passed since Earl had come for her father. It was awful when the police searched the house. It took days. Everything relating to the reno business was meticulously analyzed and finally removed. Ashley was now in the process of cleaning out her things and moving to Winnipeg. She would have to give it another "go" with her mom. It wasn't ideal but things might be better now that Dad was away. She would never get along nearly as good with the old lady—that was a given. There would be a new beginning focused in a much different direction. Melanie would come and visit the big city. It would be just like they always planned. Boxes, packing paper and tape were strewn all over the house. There were no short cuts to any move. Where were those hockey sticks? As the note instructed, Ashley opened the shed door—she reached out for the old microwave door.